"I'm a man without a past."

"I don't care about your past, Austin," Kacy told him, putting her hands once more on his chest. "I'm not a woman who plays it safe. I'm not going to let you play it safe, either."

"That sounds like a threat," Austin said, his breath a bit uneven.

"Think of it as a promise." The look in his eyes sent a shiver of delightful anticipation through her. "And, I warn you, I always keep my promises."

Dear Reader,

February is a month made for romance, and here at Harlequin American Romance we invite *you* to be our Valentine!

Every month, we bring you four reasons to celebrate romance, and beloved author Muriel Jensen has reasons of her own—*Four Reasons for Fatherhood,* to be precise. Join former workaholic Aaron Bradley as he learns about parenthood—and love—from four feisty youngsters and one determined lady in the finale to our exciting miniseries THE DADDY CLUB.

Some men just have a way with women, and our next two heroes are no exception. In Pamela Bauer's *Corporate Cowboy,* when Austin Bennett hits his head and loses his memory, Kacy Judd better watch out—because her formerly arrogant boss is suddenly the most irresistible man in town! And in *Married by Midnight* by Mollie Molay, Maxwell Taylor has more charm than even he suspects—he goes to a wedding one day, and wakes up married the next!

And if you're wondering HOW TO MARRY… *The World's Best Dad,* look no farther than Valerie Taylor's heartwarming tale. Julie Miles may not follow her own advice, but she's got gorgeous Ben Harbison's attention anyway!

We hope you enjoy every romantic minute of our four wonderful stories.

Warm wishes,

Melissa Jeglinski
Associate Senior Editor

Corporate
Cowboy

PAMELA BAUER

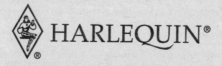

TORONTO • NEW YORK • LONDON
AMSTERDAM • PARIS • SYDNEY • HAMBURG
STOCKHOLM • ATHENS • TOKYO • MILAN • MADRID
PRAGUE • WARSAW • BUDAPEST • AUCKLAND

For two people who are very dear to me,
Kathy and Bill Greising

And to Lois Greiman, a special thanks
for answering my questions

ISBN 0-373-16814-4

CORPORATE COWBOY

Copyright © 2000 by Pamela Muelhbauer.

Visit us at www.romance.net

Printed in U.S.A.

ABOUT THE AUTHOR

Pamela Bauer was born and raised in Minnesota where you need a sense of humor if you're going to survive winter. That's why she writes romantic comedies set in the Midwest with heroes who know how to warm a woman's heart...and toes. She has received awards from *Affaire de Coeur* and *Romantic Times Magazine* and her books have appeared on the Waldenbooks romance bestseller list. She currently makes her home in Minnesota where she lives with her husband who is her real-life hero, her two adult children and a Bichon-poo who thinks he's human. When she's not writing, she enjoys watching foreign films, going to the theater and fishing.

Books by Pamela Bauer

HARLEQUIN AMERICAN ROMANCE

Don't miss any of our special offers. Write to us at the following address for information on our newest releases.

Harlequin Reader Service
U.S.: 3010 Walden Ave., P.O. Box 1325, Buffalo, NY 14269
Canadian: P.O. Box 609, Fort Erie, Ont. L2A 5X3

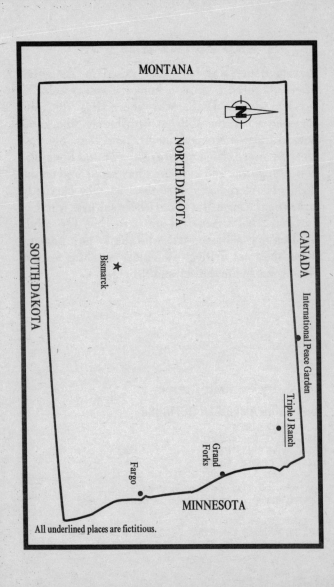

MONTANA

NORTH DAKOTA

CANADA

SOUTH DAKOTA

Bismarck

International Peace Garden

Triple J Ranch

Grand Forks

Fargo

MINNESOTA

All underlined places are fictitious.

Chapter One

"Uh-oh. You weren't able to convince them, were you?"

Austin Bennett breezed past his secretary, ignoring the stack of messages she held in her outstretched hand. "Six to one in favor of the dude ranch."

"Oh, my," Jean trailed after him, distress adding more lines to her already creased face. "I thought at least Henry..." she trailed off.

Austin groaned as he sank into his leather chair. No, not even his father had been on his side. Not that Austin had expected paternal support on this—or any other—issue. He had learned long ago that if he was going to make it in the family business it wouldn't be because his father had made it easy for him. Quite the opposite. Even after ten years working for Bennett Industries, Austin had never lost the feeling that he needed to prove himself to his father.

And lately Austin felt like a lone salmon swimming upstream. Even employees he had handpicked had suddenly became his father's advocates and his adversaries.

Austin shouldn't have expected anything different. Getting along with others had never been easy for him. According to his mother, the very first time he had crawled into a group of toddlers at the day-care center he had created a fuss. The results of grabbing a squeaking rubber hammer from a ten-month-old pacifist were all it took for him for him to realize the world didn't always look favorably upon those who went after what they wanted in life.

And Austin did go after what he wanted, often with a relentless determination he had learned from his father. It was why the two of them had always been at odds. They were two of a kind and because his father had started in an entry-level position in the furniture manufacturing firm, Austin too—even with an MBA in management—had to work his way up the ranks. With a man like Henry Bennett at the helm, it had been an uphill battle. But he'd made it. He may have stepped on a few toes along the way, but he had done what was necessary to be a success.

There was no shortage of profits for the company or its employees. What Austin lacked in people skills he made up for in acumen. And if his employees grumbled about the long hours and demanding work schedule, they never complained when he handed them their paychecks.

Even his father was the first to admit that Austin had a talent for making money. His diversifying the family firm had increased profits enormously, allowing them to expand. Now instead of one plant in suburban Chicago there were five, scattered about the Midwest. Employees of Bennett Industries not only received good wages and benefits, but profit sharing in a company that was rapidly becoming one of the most successful firms in the country. Yet despite the monetary rewards, the turnover rate was high—so high that the board of directors had come up with a solution to the problem. A management seminar designed to teach Bennett employees cutting-edge team-building techniques.

Austin had argued long and hard against the idea when it had been originally proposed and he still lobbied against it. At today's board meeting when he had been overruled in his objections to the plan, he had announced that he wouldn't be able to attend the seminar. His father had told him, in no uncertain terms, that it wasn't optional.

Austin swiveled his chair until he was facing the plate glass windows, looking out across the Chicago skyline. It didn't matter that he had the title of CEO. His father still ran Bennett Industries.

"It's a foolish idea," he mumbled.

"It might not be as bad you think," Jean consoled him in her motherly way.

"I understand the psychology of sending employees on a trip to get away from the office, but why would anyone turn down a chance to sip cocktails in the Cayman Islands to play cowboy on the prairies of North Dakota?" he pondered as he stared at the city. "The prairie!" he repeated in disbelief. He twirled around so that he was once again facing her. "Have you ever been to North Dakota, Jean?"

"No, but I hear it's quite lovely."

He grunted. "If you like flat land and grass. When I was a kid my aunt and uncle took me to visit a cousin in Montana. Six of us in a station wagon loaded down with suitcases and games, seeing the USA in our Chevrolet." He chuckled sardonically. "We drove for hours and saw nothing but a couple of grain elevators and a few clapboard buildings."

"It probably just seemed that way because you were a kid. Besides, that was a long time ago. I'm sure it's changed since then. I believe I read recently that very little of the tall grass prairie remains.''

"Well, maybe the tall grass isn't there, but the land is still flat.''

"At least you'll have peace and quiet. And according to the brochure the accommodations are quite plush,'' she said in her usual optimistic way. "The Triple J has an excellent reputation. You saw the profile they did on that news program.''

"Yes, and unfortunately so did George Harbison, which is why he brought the idea to the board. He says it's just what we need. Team building.'' The words were muttered with disgust. "I can't believe that roughing it out on the prairie is going to foster anything but irritability.''

Jean hid her smile. "I wouldn't call spending five nights in a private room with a hot tub roughing it. I'm sure it's not going to be that bad.''

"It's a ranch, Jean, not a hotel. And I don't see how pretending to be cowboys is going to teach any skills useful in the corporate world.''

"I believe the brochure called it experiential learning. You learn to work with others in risk-tasking situations and ideally, learn about yourself.''

Again Austin shook his head. "We need management strategies, not this touchy-feely crap. If you ask me, it's pouring money down the drain. Why can't everyone else see it for what it is?''

"Oh, but it's not wasted money. Didn't you read the part about there being a money-back guarantee? They're so certain of their results, they'll refund your money if you're not satisfied.''

"Time is not refundable. I'm going to lose a week of work and I don't think it's a good idea to allow fifteen of our managers to be away from the office at the same time.''

''You didn't think it was a problem for all of them to be gone at the same time when they were all at the sales conference in Phoenix last winter,'' she reminded him.

''That was different.'' He loosened his tie and undid the top button on his shirt. ''Thank goodness for laptops and fax machines. At least I will be able to stay abreast of things through the Internet.''

''Laptop? Isn't that what this whole program is about—getting away from the phones and computers and fax machines? I thought I read that you aren't supposed to bring any work with you?''

''Jean, you know I go nowhere without my laptop. Do you realize how bored I would be if I didn't bring work?''

''I believe the Triple J has a full schedule for you.''

He grunted. ''I'm not going to do this cowboy number. If I have to get on a horse and take a trail ride to show everyone I'm a team member, fine. But while they're all out mending fences or rounding up cattle or whatever else it is they're going to rope people into doing, I'll be in my room with my laptop.''

Jean arched one eyebrow. ''But the point of the getaway is to do just that—get away from the stress of your regular work.''

''Work isn't a stress for me, Jean. It's people who give me stress. And I'm taking them with me.''

''Well, hopefully you'll come home with a better understanding of those people.''

He sighed and leaned back in his chair. ''You think this corporate retreat center is a good idea, don't you?''

''It's not my place to advise you, Austin. But I do know that I've been with this firm for almost forty years and never have I seen a man who works as much as you do. Even if you get nothing else out of this, at least it will be time away from the office.''

''I'd rather be here.''

''Austin, you can't work twenty-four hours a day, seven days a week. Everyone needs a break from the office,'' she chastised him gently in a tone only she could use. ''Working the hours you do leaves little time for recreation. You haven't had a vacation in four years—and don't tell me that trip to Hong Kong with that fashion model was a vacation. You would have never gone had you not been able to close the deal with the fabric suppliers.''

''I went to Jamaica last month.''

''Business.''

''London last April.''

''Business. Austin, you need to give your mind a rest. You know what you should do? Take a few extra days when this retreat is over and visit those cousins in Montana. Forget about work. Forget about people. Just be free.''

Austin rubbed his chin thoughtfully. ''I'm not sure I know how not to work, Jean.''

''Then maybe it's time you learned. Wouldn't it be nice to retrace that car trip you took as a child—go visit those cousins, see how they've changed? I bet they'd love to hear from you.''

''I haven't seen them in over twenty years,'' he said wistfully. ''I'm not sure they're even in Montana anymore.''

''Want me to do some checking?''

''No, I shouldn't even be gone for the week at the ranch.''

Then, as she had done so often since his mother had

died, Jean sat down across from him and leaned her arms on his desk, her voice taking on a familiar maternal tone. "You're working too hard the way it is, Austin. I'm afraid one of these days I'm going to get a call saying you've worked yourself to exhaustion. Why don't I look up the names of those cousins? At least you'll have it with you and after the visit to the ranch if you find you want to take some extra time, you can do it."

He reached across the desk to gently squeeze her arm. "All right. Get me their phone numbers." He gave her a smile, then flipped open his daily planner. "About my plane reservation…"

"Jan in travel said everyone's leaving at one-thirty on Sunday afternoon."

"I don't want to go that early in the day."

"You're supposed to arrive as a group." There was admonition in her voice.

"A few hours shouldn't make a difference."

"But the idea is to begin this training as a *team*. That's the key to success."

"And when has anything I touched not been a success?" he retorted with a devilish grin. "Book me on the last available flight that day."

Before Jean could protest, the door flew open. Austin knew there was only one person who would be brave enough to enter without knocking. He glanced up to see Daphne Delattre sweep into the room in her usual dramatic way. She moved with the grace expected of a runway model, not a hair out of place, not a smudge in her perfectly made-up face. She ignored Jean and went straight to Austin, brushing her lips across his cheek.

Austin didn't miss the way his secretary cringed at the action. After a polite greeting, Jean exited, leaving Austin alone with the high fashion model, but not before casting him a disapproving look. Ever since the day his father had introduced him to Daphne, Jean had felt it was her duty to warn Austin of the dangers of a woman like Daphne Delattre.

Austin had told his secretary on several different occasions that the model was his father's choice of companions for him, not his. Judging by her attitude, she didn't believe him.

Daphne perched herself on the corner of his desk, deliberately exposing the slender thigh of one leg. "Why are you scowling? Aren't you happy to see me?"

"I'm not scowling," Austin answered. "I always look like this when I'm working."

"Then you should stop working and take me to lunch."

Austin ignored the flirtatious pose and glanced at his daily planner. "Can't do that. Schedule's full."

"You must be able to get free for at least an hour?"

"As long as I'm in the building I'm never free," he answered, grimacing as he ran a hand around the back of his neck in an attempt to work free a kink that was cramping a muscle.

She immediately hopped down off the desk and pushed away his hand, replacing it with hers. "Here. Let me."

Austin didn't protest. If there was one quality he appreciated in Daphne it was her therapeutic touch. "You know you went into the wrong profession. You should have been a masseuse."

She harrumphed in disagreement. "So are you going to tell me what has these muscles as hard as a rock?"

"No."

She made a sound of disgust. "What you need is some time away from this place."

"You sound just like Jean today."

"Well, for once I agree with her. You need a break."

"Well, you'll be happy to hear that's exactly what I'm going to get."

Her fingers stopped massaging and she turned to face him. "You're taking a vacation?" Hope danced in her eyes.

He chuckled. "No, a business trip."

"When is it? I have some time coming up. Maybe I could arrange my schedule and come with you."

Austin never mixed business and pleasure. "No, that won't work."

She stopped her kneading. "You don't want me there?"

There was a little catch in her voice, a ploy that was becoming very familiar to Austin. Daphne was not above using every feminine wile she possessed to get her way. At first Austin had found it amusing, but lately it had begun to annoy him. She played games, which was the kiss of death for any relationship with a woman as far as Austin was concerned.

About the only good thing he could say about a trip to this ranch in North Dakota was that it would put a little distance between him and Daphne. Lately she had started assuming their relationship was more serious than it was. It didn't help that his father encouraged her.

Neither one of them wanted to accept the fact that Austin wasn't ready to settle down with any woman. His father and Daphne had become a tag team whose goal was to get him to the altar.

Austin sighed. Maybe getting out of Chicago for a week wasn't such a bad idea.

KATHLEEN CHARLOTTE JUDD was not a stubborn person, although she had every right to be. It was in the Judd genes. Her grandfather, her father and both of her brothers had stubborn streaks that could try the patience of a saint. Fortunately, Kacy took after her mother's side of the family and although she could be a bit headstrong at times, the folks around Cavalier, ND, knew she had a sweet disposition which was difficult to undermine. She was also good under pressure and enjoyed working with people, which is why the Judds had put her in charge of public relations for the Triple J.

Only today she was not feeling very sweet. It had rained six of the last seven days. If the sun didn't shine soon, she would get downright cranky and not just because she needed its rays to boost her endorphins. The creeks were swollen, the ground was muddy and fifteen people were expecting to spend the next four days in the outdoors, riding, roping and rounding up cattle. It was enough to make any cowgirl edgy.

Kacy, born and raised on the ranch, was accustomed to working through not only rain, but snow, sleet and ice. The guests at the Triple J, however, didn't have her years of experience with the elements. They were urban cowboys who wanted to experience life on the ranch, which was why unless the rain stopped, the upcoming week would be one big muddy challenge.

Because it was wet, the opening dinner was served in the dining room instead of outside around a campfire. All of the staff at the Triple J wore western wear, including Kacy and her sister, Suzy, who had on long denim skirts and fringed leather vests.

Halfway through dinner, her brother Dusty said, "Someone has to go back to Grand Forks to pick up the last guest."

"What last guest?" Kacy asked warily.

He didn't so much as blink. "The one that's coming in at nine-thirty."

"This isn't the entire group?" she asked, surveying the crowd in the dining room.

"Nope. There's one more coming and someone has to go get him at the airport."

She set her fork down and fixed him with an inquisitive glare. "Since when do we make special trips for one?"

"Since it's the CEO—Mr. Austin Bennett himself."

Kacy groaned. "You should have told him to rent a car and drive out here if he couldn't come with the others."

Dusty clicked his tongue. "That's what Dad said."

"Well, for once I agree with Dad."

He rested his arm along the back of her chair and said, "Aw, come on, Kacy. You know you don't mean that. If you did you wouldn't be in charge of PR around here. You're the one who's always telling me how important it is to be accommodating."

Normally, Kacy wouldn't have argued with her brother, but today she was feeling in no mood to cater to anyone, especially not a man in a suit. "I'm sorry, Dusty, you'll have to forgive me, but I just don't feel very accommodating today."

"Aw, Kace, I know it's been a bad day, what with you getting that letter and all," he sympathized. "But you can't blame all the suits for what one man did."

She didn't. But getting a Dear John—or a "Dear Joan" letter, as her sister Suzy had called it—made her feel as if she were entitled to be just a bit irrational today. "Gran always said that on any given day you'd find at least one Judd holding a grudge against someone or something. I guess today's my day."

Dusty groaned. "Dad should never have encouraged you to go to New York."

But her father had urged her to go. Since childhood she had dreamed of living anywhere but on the ranch. She had been consumed with a need to explore the world outside of North Dakota, to soak up all the excitement she knew had to be happening in the big city. As soon as she had graduated college with her degree in art history, she went in search of that dream.

She took a job in an art gallery where she discovered that the life she had fantasized was not all she expected it to be. As she gradually became less enchanted with the bright lights of the city, she began to realize that although she loved art, what she really wanted was to be with her horses in the wide open spaces of North Dakota. After three years she had packed up her things and moved home. Her only regret about leaving the city was that she had to leave the man she loved.

At least she thought she had been in love with Steven Delancey. Now she knew that she should have ended their relationship when she had told him she was quitting her job and moving back to North Dakota.

He hadn't tried to convince her to change her mind. Instead he had acted relieved that she had made the decision to leave New York, telling her he would be able to get more work done if she wasn't around to distract him. Kacy knew now that that's all she had been—a distraction. An up-and-coming lawyer wanting to make partner in his law firm, Steven was focused—too focused. For him, work was more than a way to earn a living. It was an obsession.

No woman would ever be number one in Steven's life. Work would always come first, because his whole life centered around his profession. A wife and children would always take a back seat.

It was not the kind of life Kacy wanted—to be second fiddle to a job. And she did want marriage and a family—something she wasn't sure would ever be on Steven's agenda.

Six months ago she hadn't wanted to admit that it was over. Now she could hardly believe it had taken her this long to let it go. The only reason their relationship had lasted as long as it did was because she had made it work, not because of any effort on his part. That's why when his Dear Joan letter came she felt so angry. *He* was the one calling it quits when *she* was the one who had done all the work.

Kacy had not been happy in New York, not just because of what had happened with Steven. She knew now that it had been foolish of her to think that working in a concrete and glass world would make her happy. She needed open spaces and fresh air. For that's what was in her blood—the smell of leather and dust, the sight of cattle bunched in the corner of a pasture, waves of buffalo grass and sage, and sunsets that seemed to go on forever making one realize just how small a speck anyone is on this earth. Give her a man in jeans and boots any day over any of the suits pressing the city pavement. She preferred to live in a world of Levi's and leather rather than wool and silk.

"Didn't anybody tell this suit that the reason the program works is because it's a *team* effort? I say let him rent a car and drive out here himself," she grumbled.

"Kacy, be reasonable."

"Reasonable as in get in the van and go get him?" she asked dryly.

"Doesn't it beat reciting poetry around the camp-fire?"

"It's too wet for a campfire," she reminded him.

"Then we'll have to have poetry around the fire-place." He grinned. "Come on. Be a sport. Other than the orientation meeting, you won't be missed this evening."

Kacy knew what he said was true. She was the public relations person at the Triple J which meant she usually saw to it that guests were comfortable at all times. Her other job was to give riding lessons and lead trail rides.

"Please say you'll do it," he begged.

She tried to give him the stubborn look the Judds were noted for, but failed. "All right. But I'm not taking that big old honkin' van. I'll drive my pickup."

"You can't pick up a CEO in that beat-up old pickup!"

Kacy didn't appreciate anyone referring to Bertha as either "old" or "beat-up." "Do you want me to do it or not?"

Dusty handed her a white placard with "The Triple J" written across the front in large black letters. "You probably won't need this, but better take it anyway."

"You're lucky I have such a strong sense of family duty," she mumbled as she took the placard from him.

On her way out she grabbed a slicker from the coat room. It was a good thing because before she had reached the airport, rain fell in a steady downpour. She pulled up in front of the terminal in the loading zone, looking for signs of a suit. No one waited near the entrance.

She felt her muscles tense. For three years she had made airports a regular stop on her agenda. Her clothes had spent more time in her suitcase than her closet. Buying art for the gallery, arranging for showings, traveling cross country had all sounded glamorous to her at one point in her life.

Now she knew better. She was grateful she was no longer earning frequent flyer miles. There were no more long hours spent trying to convince a temperamental artist to agree to a showing, no more frustrating conversations with fussy patrons with outrageous demands, no more dates with men whose only goal in life is to get ahead in the business world.

Instead of worsted wool and linen, she could wear denim and leather. She was done trying to be a sophisticated city woman. In her heart she was a cowgirl and there was no point in pretending to be anything else.

Not that it mattered. Her days of doing what she was supposed to do were over…except of course when it came to the ranch. To keep the Triple J in the family, she would do anything, including cater to stuffy businessmen who didn't have a clue what it really meant to be a rancher.

Knowing she couldn't stay in the loading zone indefinitely, she drove into the parking lot. Before getting out, she buttoned up the slicker, cursing the fact that she had to get out in the pouring down rain to go find this guy. She grabbed the square Triple J placard and made a dash to the door.

It was nearly deserted inside the airport except for a couple of airline personnel. Kacy's eyes scanned the small waiting room and saw a man leaning up against the wall, his back to her as he spoke on the telephone. He wore a suit and carried a briefcase. Kacy figured it had to be Austin Bennett, the CEO of Bennett Industries.

As she walked toward him she could hear the heels of her boots clack against the floor. She expected the sound would cause him to turn around and look to see who was walking toward him. It didn't. He just kept on talking, loudly enough so that anyone in the area could have heard his end of the conversation. It didn't take Dr. Ruth to figure out that he was having a lovers' quarrel.

When she heard him say, "Of course I care about you, Daphne." Kacy's boots came to a halt.

Before she could take a step backward, she heard, "It's not a question of my feelings for you... Please don't cry. Daphne, stop. Do you think I want to spend a week with people who say yee-haw more than they do hello? Daphne?"

He pulled the receiver away from his ear and stared into the earpiece. "Damn," he muttered, then hung the phone up.

Without even seeing the man's face or speaking to him Kacy knew she wasn't going to like him. In a few phrases he seemed to have confirmed her worst feelings about men in suits. She couldn't help but wonder if Daphne was his girlfriend or his mistress.

She glanced at his hands. No rings on any of his fingers. A flash of gold showed beneath a crisp white cuff whenever he moved those hands. Probably a Rolex watch. It would go along with the Italian leather shoes and the Armani suit. And then there was his fragrance. Kacy had walked past the men's counter in Macy's department store enough times to know that it was not a cheap bottle of splash-on from the drugstore.

No, this man had money. And as much as she hated to admit it, he did smell good. Damn good. A man to avoid, Kacy thought pragmatically, although she didn't think she needed to worry about Mr. Bennett tossing his charm her way. She didn't exactly attract the corporate type nowadays.

Suddenly aware of her presence he turned and gave her an intense stare that told her he wasn't the least embarrassed that she had overheard his conversation. If anything, that gaze accused her of invading his privacy. Some women might have blushed or looked away. Kacy might have, had she been in New York City or Chicago or some other corporate metropolis, but not here. Not on her own turf.

"Yee-haw." She held up the placard with the Triple J logo on it.

His eyes—deep blue and penetrating—narrowed, making a very thorough appraisal of her figure, from her head covered by her felt cowboy hat down to her booted toes. As they traveled down the rain soaked slicker, she was grateful that he couldn't see the open slit in her skirt, for she was certain those eyes would have lingered a moment on the expanse of leg it revealed. She hadn't reached the age of twenty-six without learning how to recognize what was in a man's eyes. As much as she'd like to give him an icy glare, she stepped toward him, hand outstretched.

"You must be Mr. Bennett. I'm Kacy Judd. Welcome to North Dakota."

He took her hand, his blue eyes continuing to pierce hers with an intensity that made every red curl beneath her hat want to straighten. Just as quickly as he had clasped her hand, he dropped it, causing Kacy to wonder if he had experienced the same jolt as she had when their skin had touched.

"Where's your luggage?" she asked.

He made a sound of derision. "It's lost. Apparently it didn't make the connecting flight in Minneapolis."

"Oh." Inwardly, Kacy smiled. It served him right. "No need to worry. I'm sure someone from the airlines will bring it to the ranch when it gets here. Until then, you can pick up a few things in the Triple J's western wear shop."

From the look on his face she doubted that he wanted to wear anything that had the word "western" connected to it. He didn't look happy and as they passed the baggage claim area Kacy gave the clerk a sympathetic glance. No doubt Mr. Austin Bennett had made sure she understood his predicament.

Judging by the look on the CEO's face, Kacy thought it would be wise for anyone to avoid talking to the man if possible. Not a friendly word had dropped from his lips yet. She could only imagine what the long ride back to the ranch was going to be like. Everything about his body language told her he didn't want to be here.

When her father and brothers had announced they wanted to convert the ranch to a conference center for professionals, Kacy had laughed out loud. Despite the fact that one of her brothers had a business degree and the other had one in psychology, neither one excelled in the public relations department.

Which was why they needed her to be a part of the family business. When it came to smoothing ruffled feathers, Kacy was a pro. After three years in New York and encountering what she thought had to be the crankiest people on the face of the earth, working with professionals hoping to find better methods of communicating was a piece of cake.

Only this piece of cake looked as if someone could break a tooth if they tried to do anything but stay out of his way. He was going to be a challenge and although it would be easy to avoid Austin Bennett, Kacy was not one to run away from a job she was supposed to do. One way or another, she'd get this city slicker saying "yee-haw" before the week was over.

Chapter Two

"I don't suppose you have an umbrella in that, do you?" Kacy pointed to his briefcase. "It's coming down pretty good out there."

Austin thought pretty good was an understatement. The road out front looked like a river. "It wasn't raining when I left Chicago."

"I take it that's a no."

"Considering the prices your facility charges, Ms. Judd, one would expect that umbrellas would be provided for guests by the Triple J." Austin didn't mean to snap at the woman, but he didn't care for the censure in her tone. After his conversation with Daphne, he wasn't in the mood to be defending himself to any woman.

And especially not this one. His gaze slid over her again, wondering just what kind of a place would send a woman wearing cowboy boots, a cowboy hat and a yellow rain slicker better suited to a two-hundred-pound firefighter.

"Oh, but we do provide umbrellas, Mr. Bennett. All of your employees who came on time were greeted with an umbrella escort. We carry them in the vans."

"But you didn't come in a van?"

"Uh-uh. I drive that orange pickup that's in the front row of the parking lot."

He glanced outside and noticed an orangish blur which he knew had to be the truck. Running even a short distance would leave him with a drenched suit. Not a pleasant thought especially since he had no change of clothes.

"I think it would be more prudent to wait a few minutes," he advised.

"Don't want to get your fancy suit wet, eh?" She gave him an understanding grin. "All right. You wait here. I'll bring the truck to the door."

"That won't be necessary. I can walk out with you, although I don't see why we can't wait until it isn't raining quite so hard." He could feel his patience slipping away.

She shrugged. "It's only water, but if you want to wait, that's fine with me. I should tell you, though, that the way it's been raining here lately, who knows when it'll clear. And the longer we stay here, the less time you'll have to spend with your employees when we get back."

"I'm sure my employees can get along without me this evening," he retorted smoothly.

"That may be true, but it is a long drive back to the ranch, Mr. Bennett, and it's already late." She reached for the door. "You're the guest, I'm the driver. You wait here. I'll get the truck."

"I'm not having you pick me up at the door!"

"Why not?"

"Because I'm not." He unzipped his briefcase to get a section of the newspaper to use as protection from the rain.

"Is that a laptop?" Kacy asked, peering over his shoulder.

"Yes." He pulled out the business section of the *Chicago Sunday Times,* aware of her eyes watching him closely.

"Now that's a shame."

"What is?"

"That you brought your PC in that carry-on. You could have packed a change of clothes. Most people do that—pack an extra set of clothes just in case the luggage goes astray."

Austin wondered if she was deliberately trying to annoy him or if he was simply in a bad mood because number one, he didn't want to be here and number two, he had just argued with Daphne. "I'm not most people and I happen to need my laptop."

"Not at the ranch you don't. You're going to be unplugged while you're there."

"Unplugged?"

"Yes. No telephones, no faxes, no PCs. This isn't a working vacation, Mr. Bennett. It's a team-building workshop that requires all of your attention and concentration."

He sighed impatiently. "Ms. Judd, I am the CEO of Bennett Industries. I have responsibilities. It would be not only foolish, but inconsiderate, for me to lose my connection with my office."

"Well, that may be, Mr. Bennett, but I think it would be even more foolish and inconsiderate of you to waste company money—which is what you will be doing if you don't give your one hundred percent to the program."

"Excuse me?" Did she honestly think that running around playing cowboy was more important than running one of the country's most successful manufacturing industries?

"This whole concept is based on teamwork. You and your fellow employees are going to have to rely on each other. You're not their CEO while you're here, just another member of the team. And as a member of the team you need to work hard so that the others will know that they can count on you. Your attention needs to be with them, not with a bunch of suits in Chicago."

Austin could only stare at her in disbelief. He ran one of the most successful manufacturing companies in the country and he was being given a lecture on management by a woman wearing cowboy boots, a yellow rubber slicker and a ten-gallon hat. What had his father gotten him into?

She peeked her nose out the door, then turned back to him and said, "I think there's a slight lull in the rainfall. We'd better leave while we can."

If this was a lull, he shuddered to think what a downpour would be. By the time Austin reached the pickup he was soaked. His hair, his face, his hands—everything dripped with water, including his briefcase. The section of the *Times* that had acted as an umbrella was a soggy mess and had done little to shield him from the driving rain. Now it fell apart, clinging to his wet fingers as he tried to shake them free.

"Do you want me to put the heat on so you can dry off a bit?" she asked as she climbed in beside him.

"I'm not cold. I'm wet," he said stiffly.

Again she shrugged. "Very well." She stuck the key in the ignition and started up the engine. "Fasten your seat belt. Next stop the Triple J."

As she let out the clutch, the truck lunged forward.

"Sorry. Sometimes the pedal sticks," she explained

with a sly grin which only raised Austin's suspicions about the sincerity of her apology. "You ever been to North Dakota before Mr. Bennett?" she asked once they were out of the parking lot and on their way.

"Once."

"And?"

"It was a long time ago."

"Well, what did you think?"

"That there's a lot of flat land," he said dully.

She chuckled. "Don't tell me you're one of those people who think the two best things about North Dakota are the east and west ends of Interstate 94?"

"Is that supposed to be a joke?"

"Of course it's a joke. Interstate 94 runs smack dab through the middle of the state from Minnesota to Montana. It implies there's nothing in between the borders, which couldn't be further from the truth. It's true that much of the state is flat farmland, but if you haven't been to the northeast corner, you're in for a treat. There's the Pembina Gorge which is a beautiful river valley and there's even a ski resort. Most people..."

He quickly cut her off. "You can save yourself the bother of giving me the guided tour, Ms. Judd."

"You don't want to hear what your colleagues already heard?" she asked in an annoying innocent tone.

"I'm sure North Dakota has an abundance of natural wonders, but right now I'm wet, I have no change of clothing and I don't feel up to hearing a travelogue of your state," he snapped.

"You should have let me pick you up at the door." She had the audacity to scold him cheerfully.

Before he could utter another word his cellular phone rang. As he pulled it out of his pocket, he heard Kacy click her tongue in admonition. He shot her a nasty look before answering the call. "Yes?"

It was Daphne, hoping to continue the phone conversation he had started at the airport.

"I can't believe you hung up on me like that!" Her voice was so loud Austin had to wonder if Kacy didn't hear it, too.

"This isn't a good time for me to talk. Go to bed. I'll call you in the morning," he said quietly into the pocket-sized phone.

"I'm not going to let you cast me aside like some used piece of furniture," Daphne continued to shout into the phone.

"I'm not doing that. All I'm saying is this is not a good time to talk."

"But we need to discuss our feelings."

Feelings were something Austin rarely discussed with anyone. And certainly not in the presence of a cowgirl.

"Daphne, please," he pleaded, but she refused to be deterred. Fortunately, they were driving out of range of the transmission and her voice became weaker. Finally he said, "I can't hear you, Daphne. I'm going to have to hang up and talk to you when I'm not in transit." He said goodbye and tucked the phone back into his pocket.

A glance told him Kacy sat with a smug smile of satisfaction—as if she knew he wasn't going to be able to get any reception on the phone and was pleased about it.

"Satisfied?" he asked churlishly, wondering what it was about the woman sitting next to him that made him want to reach across and kiss that smile right off her pretty little face.

And it was a pretty face. At least what he could see of it. Cute bow lips highlighted with just the faintest of red lipstick, a pert little nose, a dainty but determined chin. And green eyes that he swore sparkled with mischief. She didn't have the kind of looks that made the runway models famous, but she was pretty.

Of course he couldn't see her forehead. Maybe she had one of those apelike brows that would erase the beauty of the rest of her face. That could be why she wore the hat—to cover up a bad hairline.

He chuckled. Who was he kidding? She was cute, in a country sort of way. Not that it mattered to him. He hadn't come to North Dakota looking for Daphne's replacement. At the thought of the model he sighed. He should have broken it off with her weeks ago. The relationship was going nowhere. Kacy Judd must have mistaken the meaning of his sigh.

"If you need to make emergency calls, we do have phones at the ranch," she said politely.

"Do I have to be bleeding to use one?" He couldn't keep the sarcasm from his voice.

"We don't want to completely isolate you, Mr. Bennett," she continued in her annoying calm voice, "but the team approach is much more effective if there are no phone interruptions. Of course we understand that there are times when you may need to touch base with your family."

Family? What he needed to keep in touch with was work, not family. Although in his case, the two were unfortunately connected. If there was anything positive to be said about the trip to North Dakota it was that he would get a break from people who seemed hellbent upon making his life stressful.

He leaned his head back and closed his eyes. He really was tired. Maybe a week at a ranch wouldn't be so bad after all. He could get some much needed rest as well as work without any interruptions. Mentally he prepared the upcoming week, assessing the pending reports, letting the sounds of the tires rotating over the pavement lull him into a state of relaxation.

How long they traveled in silence he wasn't sure. His peace was shattered at the sound of tires squealing on pavement and a horn blaring. Austin's eyes flew open to discover they had come to a stop only inches in front of the biggest moose he had ever seen. Actually, it might have been the only moose he had ever seen.

The creature seemed to be in no hurry to move from the highway. It was almost as if it took a wicked pleasure in blocking the road.

Kacy leaned her head on her steering wheel and let out a long gasp of air. "That was too close for comfort."

Much too close thought Austin, watching the moose sniff the hood of the pickup, as if expecting to find dinner. It snorted, causing Austin to sit back as far as possible in the truck.

Kacy again tooted the horn, but the animal seemed oblivious to the noise.

"It's not moving," Austin stated inanely.

"No foolin'."

"Why isn't it moving?"

"Because moose don't move for anyone or anything. They don't have to."

He hoped she was joking, but he could see by the caution on her face that she wasn't. "Now what?"

"Now we wait until it moves out of our way."

"You can't just back up and drive around it?"

"It's best not to try to outsmart a moose."

"You're pulling my leg, right?"

She shot him a sideways glance. "Messing with a moose is no joking matter, Mr. Bennett and it's something you should remember should you find yourself face to face with one while you're here. Bullwinkle may be sweet and lovable, but the moose out here can be mean, nasty creatures.''

As if to prove her point, the large animal nudged the front end of the truck with his rack, causing Kacy to cuss. ''Damn! I hope he doesn't dent my front end.''

Austin wasn't so much worried about the truck as he was about the two of them inside. He wasn't sure if humans could outrun moose.

Finally, after what seemed to Austin to be an eternity, the animal backed away from the pickup and sauntered over to the shoulder of the highway where he paused to give them another look before ambling away. Kacy put the truck in gear and her foot on the gas pedal. As they sped down the highway she hummed as if she hadn't a care in the world.

After a few minutes, Austin asked, ''Does that happen often?''

''What? Moose blocking the road? Every now and then. It's a good thing we weren't talking, otherwise I might not have noticed it when I did.''

Austin decided it would better not to engage her in conversation and went silent. She, however, didn't seem to be as concerned.

''You ever see the damage a deer can do when it hits a car?'' She didn't wait for him to respond but continued on, ''Well, that animal weighs about twice as much as any deer, maybe even three times. And moose have longer legs which means a higher center of gravity so they often come right through the windshield. Did you ever see that movie with Geena Davis where that deer came crashing right through the windshield? It's not a pretty sight.''

And one Austin didn't care to visualize. He wondered where help would come from if they were to have an accident or even break down. In the entire time they'd been driving, they hadn't passed a single car. "Is it always this dark along this highway?"

"You're not in Chicago, Mr. Bennett. This is North Dakota. You're lucky we have a paved road…and that's coming to an end before long." Was that pleasure he heard in her voice?

Austin wasn't sure which was worse—riding with his eyes wide open and watching for a critter to leap out of the darkness or sitting with his eyes shut and waiting for her to slam on her brakes. In the beam of the headlights he could see all sorts of flying insects and occasionally one would plop against the windshield.

What was he doing here? he asked himself, growing more restless by the minute. He wasn't a nature lover and he certainly had no affinity for the wide open spaces. He was a city boy, born and bred, and while other people complained of the congestion and noise, he thrived on it.

"You know, you look awfully tense sitting there clutching your briefcase. You can lean back and close your eyes. I won't run us off the road."

Easier said than done, Austin thought. "How much farther is it?"

"We're almost there."

A short while later Austin realized that *almost* in North Dakota was not the same as *almost* in Chicago. Just as she predicted, the pavement gave way to a gravel road which she drove across at an alarming speed. He could hear rocks hit the underside of the pickup and was tempted to plead with her to slow down. Instead he gritted his teeth and sucked on his horehound drops.

By the time they reached the ranch the rain finally stopped. As she drove through an iron gate arched with the words "The Triple J," Austin could see a smattering of lights in the distance.

"Am I going to be able to get a change of clothing at this hour?" he asked.

"My sister Suzy runs the western wear shop. She's probably still hanging around the lodge, but even if she isn't there, I can let you in."

The closer they got to the conference center, the less apprehensive Austin became. The building she referred to as the lodge was made out of logs, giving it a very rustic look. At first glance it appeared to be long and narrow, but as she drove around the side he saw that it was actually L-shaped.

"Here we are. Welcome to the Triple J Guest House," Kacy said as she pulled up under a large canopy. "We'll check you in at the front desk, get your room key and then we'll go look for Suzy to see about getting you some clothes."

Austin nodded and followed her inside where the decor was definitely a style befitting a dude ranch. Dark paneling, thick beams and coach lanterns on the walls gave one the feeling of stepping back in time to the old west.

Kacy walked ahead of him, sliding her arms out of the slicker as she moved, thereby giving Austin a bit of a surprise. The body beneath the rubber rain coat was as near perfection as any he'd seen. She wore a long denim skirt that was unbuttoned to the knees revealing a most attractive pair of legs. But it was the leather vest that garnered his attention. It clung to her bosom in a most delectable manner and brought to his attention that despite the initial tomboy impression she had given him, she was all woman.

She hung the slicker on a wooden coat tree that had antlers for hooks, then led him to the front desk in the lobby. In keeping with the decor, a hitching post separated the guests from the employees.

"Normally there's someone working here, but I think everyone's in the lounge listening to Wild Bill Bordon. It's not often we get a man of his fame here." Slipping behind one of the posts, she unlocked a drawer and pulled out a ledger, flipping through the pages until she found what she was looking for.

"You're in number ten—a private, as you requested." She had him sign several forms, gave him a folder containing the schedule for the upcoming week, then handed him a key.

She checked for messages in the row of wooden boxes behind her on the wall, pulling out a stack of pink slips which she handed to Austin. "Someone's been trying to reach you. A Daphne Delattre. I guess you didn't tell her that you're not supposed to get phone calls here, did you?" Her delicate brow arched with a hint of impatience.

He shoved the messages into his pocket without any explanation, knowing perfectly well that she had heard his phone conversation in the truck.

"The first thing I'd like to do is get a change of clothing," he stated in no uncertain terms.

"Suzy is probably at the campfire…or I should say in front of the fireplace. We had to move the cowboy poetry reading that should have been outside around a campfire indoors."

"Oh, what a shame that I missed it." He didn't try to hide his sarcasm.

"You don't like poetry, Mr. Bennett?"

"I'm just wondering what makes poetry *cowboy* poetry?"

"Why, when it's about the life of cowboys," she said with an engaging grin. "And tonight we have one of the best poets in the West—Wild Bill Bordon."

A man named Wild Bill reading poetry? He had never been a fan of poetry readings when they were done by literary figures, but to listen to a cowboy reading poetry? Austin could feel his discomfort level rise.

"Wild Bill puts so much energy and emotion into his readings his poems become quite powerful," she told him. "If you've never been to a cowboy poetry reading you're in for quite a treat."

Austin studied her face to see if she was being facetious. She wasn't. She truly thought that some guy sitting around reciting rhymes about horses and cattle would be an engaging experience. "I'll pass on the poetry reading," he told her.

He saw a flicker of annoyance cross her face, but it was quickly replaced with a cajoling grin and a wagging of her finger at him. "Uh-uh-uh. That is no way to start the program, Mr. Bennett. Come on. This is a great way to get into the western theme of the conference." She steered him down a corridor lined with portraits and landscapes, all featuring cowboys.

"You like art, Mr. Bennett?" she asked, noting his interest.

"As a matter of fact I do." He paused in front of a painting of an elderly man wearing a buckskin jacket. The brass plate at the bottom of the frame read James Judd. "Is this your grandfather?"

"Great-grandfather. He was eighty-nine when that was done." He would have liked to ask her who the rest of the faces were on the walls, but she again was nudging him along.

"You'll have more time in the morning to look at these. Right now we need to find the rest of your group. Your employees will be eager to see that you've arrived safely. Besides, it's where we'll find Suzy and you do want to get a change of clothes for tomorrow, don't you?"

She had him over a barrel. Reluctantly he allowed her to escort him to a lounge in which one entire wall was a huge rock fireplace. Several leather sofas and large overstuffed recliners provided comfortable seating while a large wagon wheel chandelier glowed overhead, giving off just enough light so that the room had a warm glow.

Everyone was silent except for the toughened old cowboy who sat on a stool in front of the fireplace reciting poetry. Although a few guests chose the leather furniture, most sat on the floor forming a semicircle around the poet. Instead of their usual business clothes all of them wore western wear.

To Austin they looked like a bunch of dimestore cowboys in their stiff jeans, yoked shirts, leather boots and straw hats. What was even more surprising was that every one of them appeared to be enjoying the verses the old man recited in a voice as raspy as sandpaper. The only other sound in the room was the crackling of the wood in the fire.

As soon as the poem came to an end, Wild Bill looked over at the newcomers and nodded. All the cowboy hats turned in Austin's direction and suddenly Austin felt like the odd man out. Not only was his suit wet and wrinkled, it was totally out of place in this setting.

"Well, now. It looks like the head honcho has finally arrived," the weathered-looking old man commented.

The circle opened with several guests motioning for Austin to come sit beside them. "Are you going to join us?"

"I'd like to, but I need to get something to wear. My luggage is somewhere between here and Chicago."

A collective sigh could be heard and a blonde jumped up. She was dressed like Kacy Judd in a long denim skirt and a leather vest.

"It won't matter. We've got plenty of things for you to choose from, don't we, Kacy. You want me to open the shop?" she asked Austin, confirming his suspicion that she was indeed another one of the Judds.

"I would appreciate it."

Kacy then introduced the woman as her sister, Suzy Judd. As she smiled at Austin, he could see the resemblance between the two. Although their coloring was quite different, they had the same green eyes and a bone structure that many women would envy.

"As you can see, most everyone's already done some shopping," Suzy said with a grin, waving her hand in the direction of the other guests. Then she turned to Kacy and asked, "Are you going to come along or do you want to stay and listen to Wild Bill?"

"I'll stay here. I need to talk to Dusty anyway." Kacy extended her hand to Austin, giving him all the polite phrases, but he could see that she was about as sincere as a con man. She couldn't wait to pass him off to her sister. And that thought annoyed him.

He didn't know what role Ms. Kacy Judd was going to play in his life for the next five days, but of one thing he was certain. If she thought she was going to tell him what to do and when to do it, she was sadly mistaken.

THE FOLLOWING MORNING Kacy was up bright and early.
On mornings when there were no guests at the lodge she
began each day with a ride. Today she would be giving
riding lessons so she would wait to have the pleasure of
taking out one of her own horses.

Horses were Kacy's passion and she never grew tired
of being around them. Riding was an experience that
satisfied all of her senses. She could feel the wind on
her face, smell the grass beneath her and hear the sounds
of silence. The steady rhythm of her horse's hooves was
like music to her ear and it was what she had missed
most when she had lived in the city.

Riding was like breathing—she needed to do it reg-
ularly or she was in trouble. On the North Dakota prairie
she could ride without worry that she'd encounter some
unsavory character around the next bend. Living in New
York she had discovered what it meant to feel unsafe.
The two-legged animals walking the streets were much
more dangerous than the four-legged kind she encountered on the prairie.

She thought of how startled Austin Bennett had
looked at the sight of the moose on the highway and
smiled. His visit to North Dakota had not gotten off on
a very good start. Losing his luggage, fighting with his
girlfriend, getting soaked in the rain. She should have
had more sympathy for him, but he was a suit. And an
arrogant one at that, judging by last night. Thinking
everyone in North Dakota ran around saying "yee-
haw." Daphne Delattre was welcome to him.

Kacy couldn't help but be curious as to what kind of
woman would be attracted to a man like Austin Bennett.
Sure, he was good-looking, but he didn't have a person-
ality. That much was obvious. And no sense of humor.

And he liked to tell women what to do. *Go to bed?* Geesh! What did he think? That he was Daphne's father?

At the direction her thoughts were taking, she chastised herself, annoyed that he aroused the least bit of curiosity in her. Just because he had a couple of physical attributes that might make a woman's heart beat a little faster didn't mean she had to fantasize about the man's love life.

Maybe some women went for the arrogant type, but she wasn't one of them. She didn't mind a man with a "take charge" attitude, but she didn't need anyone telling her what to do. She pushed all thoughts of the CEO aside and prepared for the day ahead.

By the time she had showered and dressed, blue skies and sunshine alleviated her worries that they would be troubled by rain again today. Normally she would have had a quick bite of breakfast in her own kitchen, but because it was the first day of a new session at the ranch, she joined the rest of the staff for breakfast in the lodge's dining room.

Suzy, besides running the clothing shop, acted as hostess for all meals, arranging the seating and welcoming guests as they arrived. It came as no surprise to Kacy to find that her sister's place card was next to Austin Bennett's. What did come as a surprise was to see the CEO in blue jeans, a shirt with pearl snaps and a pair of oxfords. Kacy had to stifle a giggle. Dress shoes with blue jeans?

When his eyes met hers, he nodded. It was the only sign that he noticed her presence. Even though he appeared to be listening to Suzy, Kacy thought he looked detached, almost bored by everything that was going on around him. The impression only increased her antagonism toward the man.

When breakfast was over, Kacy found herself face to face with him as she left the dining room. "Good morning, Mr. Bennett. Did you sleep well?"

"Yes, I did."

"And is the room to your satisfaction?"

"The room is quite nice. Thank you."

One point in our favor, Kacy thought. She looked down at his shoes and asked, "Didn't they have boots in your size?"

"I didn't ask."

"You have some in your luggage, is that it?"

"No."

"Then what are you planning to wear for riding? You'll ruin those expensive Italian leather shoes if you wear them."

"I'm not getting on a horse, Ms. Judd."

"Riding is part of the program, Mr. Bennett," she explained calmly.

"That may be, but *I* am not riding. Now if you'll excuse me." Before she could say another word, he had turned and was walking down the corridor leading to the guest rooms.

She had been dismissed! Kacy could feel her blood pressure rising and she was tempted to go after him and let him know just who was running the show. But she didn't. She simply smiled to herself.

Let him think what he wanted. There was no way some city guy in a suit was going to get the upper hand on her. He'd learn that soon enough.

BENNETT INDUSTRIES HAD enrolled fifteen employees in the program. That meant Kacy and her brothers each worked with a team of five. When it was time for the first scheduled activity—the riding lessons—Kacy only counted four people in her group.

"Who's missing?" a man named Ed asked, shading his eyes as he glanced to the opposite corners of the corral where the rest of the participants sat on bales of hay awaiting instructions.

"It's Mr. Bennett," Kacy answered, looking at the slip of paper Dusty had handed her only minutes before.

"I didn't think he'd be out here with the rest of us," another man chipped in.

Kacy looked toward the lodge and felt a twinge of irritation which quickly escalated into a knot of anger when she saw a man walk out of the lodge and head for the pool. She didn't need a pair of binoculars to know that it was Austin Bennett. Why had the man even bothered to come to the ranch?

Determined to stay cool with the situation, she said, "Maybe Mr. Bennett doesn't need a riding lesson."

"It's more likely he doesn't want one," someone supplied.

Ed grinned. "Rumor has it that he wasn't too gung ho about coming here."

"Really?" Kacy stated innocently, knowing perfectly well Austin Bennett didn't want to be anywhere near the ranch. "But we're going to have so much fun." She wiggled her eyebrows as she grinned.

"Some of us are a little shy around horses," another guest admitted.

"There's no need to be," Kacy assured everyone. "Riding is an essential component of the work you will do here. And it's fun. So, I'll go have a little chat with Mr. Bennett. In the meantime, you can admire Harriet." She walked over to the fence and lovingly stroked a chestnut mare tied to fence. "She's a real sweetie. Wouldn't hurt a fly."

"Is everyone going to get a horse to ride?" Ed asked as she started for the pool area.

"Oh, yes. We've enough horses for everyone. Even Mr. Bennett," she said with confidence before heading toward the lodge.

Chapter Three

Most guests at the ranch used the pool area for relaxation. Not Austin Bennett. In the time it had taken Kacy to walk back from the corral he had set up a portable office on one of the round glass-topped tables in the shade of an umbrella and appeared to be hard at work.

"Mr. Bennett, what are you doing?"

He lifted his head to glance at her briefly, a pair of dark sunglasses masking his penetrating blue eyes. "I'm working, Ms. Judd."

"You're supposed to be part of a group riding lesson. Your team members are waiting for you."

"I believe I already told you I'm not getting on a horse." He kept his eyes on the computer screen, continuing to punch keys while they talked.

She felt like snatching that laptop from his hands and tossing it into the pool. Instead she took a deep breath and counted to ten. "Then you're going to have trouble keeping up with your employees. Nearly every activity at the ranch involves riding."

The gentle breeze sent a whiff of his aftershave in her direction, teasing her nostrils, increasing her awareness of him as a man. Not that she needed the heady scent to remind her of how masculine he was. He was one of the sexiest men she had ever encountered. It was a good thing he was a suit. Otherwise she could find herself easily distracted from the job at hand.

He stopped typing and glanced up at her. "Looks like I'll get more work done than I expected," he said evenly, then he smiled at her.

The smile caused her heart to skip a beat and Kacy knew she was wrong about not being distracted. "The program's been designed for fifteen people."

"Surely you can make it fifteen minus one."

"No, everything's already set up."

"Then you'll have to adjust to one less."

She had heard that tone of voice often when dealing with difficult customers at the art gallery. It said, "I'm the customer and I'm always right." Kacy could feel her patience blowing away with the wind.

"Why did you choose the Triple J for your team-building sessions if you had no intention of taking part in the program?" she asked, her hands on her hips.

"I didn't choose it."

So he had been strongarmed by bigger brass to attend. He didn't want to be at the ranch and was only there because he had no other choice. Kacy should have realized that last night when he had shown so little interest in anything she said.

Well, it wasn't the first time she had a reluctant guest at the ranch. Usually with a bit of cajoling and patience, she could get even the crankiest to join in the group activities. However, Austin Bennett didn't appear to want to have his mind changed. He looked as if he had already decided what his morning was going to involve and it wasn't horses.

"I know this isn't a typical business conference setting, but experience has shown us that often the most skeptical of guests leaves as the biggest proponents of the program,'' she said cheerfully.

''You're telling me that everyone leaves here a happy cowboy?''

''Yes. I know a trip to North Dakota doesn't sound like much of a perk, but if you'll just give us a chance, we'll see that you leave with a sense of accomplishment you never expected you'd find on the prairie,'' she promised.

''That's fine. You do your job with my employees and I'll take back a group of contented employees,'' he said smoothly.

She struggled to stay positive and not let him upset her. ''But we want you to be content, too.''

That remark brought him to his feet. He pulled off his sunglasses and pinned her with his blue eyes. ''And you think you know what makes me content, Ms. Judd?''

This time Kacy's heart didn't just skip a beat, it darn near turned over in her chest. There was no mistaking the look in those eyes. It was a challenge, and not just a professional one. Ever since she had met him at the airport last night there had been a tension between them. And she'd have to be as dumb as dirt not to recognize that it wasn't solely based on his reluctance to come to the Triple J.

The fact that he could produce an wanted physical reaction in her made her lose a bit of the self-control she had always took great pride in maintaining. ''I know my job, Mr. Bennett, and I know the results we achieve at the ranch. Now if you'd rather not join the rest of your employees, that's your choice. But I do think you should remember the agreement you signed.''

That caused his brow to crease. ''What agreement?''

''The one that says by enrolling in the program you

agree to be a willing participant in all activities unless for medical reasons you are forced to abstain. Is there a medical reason why you can't get on a horse, Mr. Bennett?''

He chuckled. "I never signed such an agreement."

"You wouldn't be here right now if you hadn't. Want me to get your registration form from the office?" she asked, giving him a smile that said "I got you on this one."

He took a step closer to her. "Maybe I did sign your form. So?"

So she didn't have him. They both knew the contract was done more in good faith than anything else. Again there was that same challenging look in his eyes, the one that sent a shiver of excitement down Kacy's spine. She forced herself to remember she was representing the Triple J, that the only reason she was standing next to this man was because of her work.

"Being a successful executive, you know that the success of any program depends on the cooperation of the individuals involved. What we do is to create original, out-of-the-ordinary experiences that bring people together. The key is to work together as a group or you defeat the purpose of being here."

She could see by the expression on her face that she hadn't convinced him. She tried another approach. "Mr. Bennett, you're obviously a hard-working, dedicated man. You wouldn't have brought all of this with you if you weren't." She waved her arm over his makeshift workplace. "All I'm asking is that you put that dedication and hard work to use here at the ranch. These are *your* employees. Some of them weren't exactly crazy about coming here, but they're all here and they're giving the program a chance to succeed."

He didn't speak for several moments, but looked toward the corral, where the other team members sat on bales of hay waiting to begin their lessons. Seeing the direction of his gaze she said, "The Triple J doesn't force its guests to do anything they don't want to do, but I really do encourage you to give the program a try."

"And if I don't?"

"You're not cheating me, Mr. Bennett. Just them."

"I'd hardly call not riding a horse cheating my employees. I'm sure they can play cowboys just fine without me," he said dryly.

"There's a little bit more to this program than playing cowboys. It's about building better people skills and judging by the way you've behaved ever since you arrived, I'd say you could use a little help in that direction." The moment she said the words, she regretted them. What she didn't need to do was insult a guest.

Only Austin Bennett wasn't insulted. "And just how do you plan to help me with my *people* skills?" he asked with a bit of amusement in his eyes.

Before she could answer his cell phone rang.

"If you'll excuse me, this is an important call," he said as he reached for the pocket-sized phone.

Once again he was dismissing her. Kacy could have cheerfully given him a swift kick with her boot. Fortunately, sanity prevailed and instead of saying more things she'd regret, she swallowed back all the nasty things she wanted to say and told him, "Very well, Mr. Bennett. However, if you change your mind about the riding lessons, you know where to find us."

Fortunately, the walk back to the corral dissolved her anger. And within a few minutes of doing what she loved best—working with the horses—she forgot all about her encounter with their difficult guest.

As soon as everyone had learned how to saddle a horse, Kacy demonstrated the basics of mounting and dismounting. None of her students had ever ridden, which actually made it easier for her, since there were no bad habits to correct. They were all eager to learn which made her realize how different the session would have been had Austin Bennett been a part of the group. His very presence would have created tension, since she couldn't get within five feet of the guy without having every nerve in her body aware of him.

As soon as the riding lessons were over, the three teams became one large group with Kacy's brothers in charge. The first team-building assignment was fence building. As everyone worked together digging post holes and setting timbers in place, Kacy thought about the man back at the pool. Not only was he missing the pleasure of riding, but the physical exertion of working together with his employees.

Even if he hadn't wanted to be a part of the program, Kacy could hardly believe that he would write off its merits without so much as even giving it a try. Without participating in even one activity he had decided it wasn't worthy of his attention.

By lunchtime she was feeling less than charitable toward the man and she sensed that his employees weren't exactly thrilled that they were dusty and sore while he looked as cool as a cucumber. Not that it mattered to Austin. He said little at lunch and Kacy wondered if his thoughts weren't on the mysterious Daphne, whom Suzy informed her had called at least half a dozen times that morning.

For the afternoon session the group was to be divided in two groups. One half would ride fence, checking for downed wire. The other would ride to a neighboring ranch where they would learn to sheer sheep. As soon as lunch was finished, Kacy approached the CEO.

"You're assigned to group two, Mr. Bennett. That's the one doing the sheep shearing," she told him.

"Do I look like I want to even get near a sheep, Ms. Judd?" he asked and Kacy's blood pressure again soared.

"Then I guess you're going to be one hungry man."

"What does sheep shearing have to do with eating? Don't tell me hunt and kill is part of the lesson," he said with a chuckle of disbelief.

"No, it isn't," she denied vigorously. "What I meant is that if you're not with us you'll miss dinner because it's served at the chuckwagon out on the range. That's why you need to come along this afternoon. We won't be returning to the lodge until after we've eaten."

His look was guarded. "I'll think about it."

"You have about forty-five minutes. That's when we meet outside."

As she expected, he was nowhere around when they met at the corral. Kacy pursed her lips and looked back at the lodge. He wasn't outside at the pool. She figured he was probably sitting inside the air-conditioned room talking to Daphne on the phone.

Kacy didn't understand why it should bother her at all. Whether or not he took part in the activities was no reflection on her skills as a facilitator, yet she felt as if he were affronting her by not showing up. The less she saw of him, the more he seemed to irritate her. Yet when she did see him, he irritated her, too. The only way she was ever going to get any peace of mind was for him to be gone. Four more days and she would never have to see Austin Bennett again. It was a thought she kept foremost in her mind.

"WE'RE SORRY, but all circuits are busy."

Austin slammed down the receiver of the telephone and sighed. He was beginning to wonder how many long distance circuits they *had* in North Dakota. Every time he tried to make a long-distance call he got the same recorded message. Or was it simply a gimmick orchestrated by the Triple J to keep guests from using the phone? After all, he was supposed to be "unplugged" at the ranch.

Austin paced about his luxurious room. With the exception of the phone service, the accommodations were on par with any five-star hotel. The problem was, he was hungry. He should have gone with the group today just to get dinner. Irritation also gnawed his insides at the memory of how Kacy Judd had returned wearing that smug look on her face, boasting of the two-inch-thick steaks they had enjoyed. His mouth watered at the thought of a slice of beef right now.

It was barely nine o'clock, yet the Bennett employees had turned in for the night. Austin didn't blame them. They had looked dog-tired when they had returned and he had felt a twinge of guilt. He probably should have gone with them, but he had a stack of reports needing his attention—reports that would make a difference for the future of Bennett Industries.

Again pangs of hunger rumbled in his stomach. There was only one thing to do. Invade the twenty-four-hour kitchen. He grabbed his room key and headed for the cafeteria.

One fluorescent bulb beamed a welcome sign at the entrance to the dining room. Austin walked through the vacant room until he reached the swing doors separating the kitchen from the dining room. As he stepped inside, he flipped a switch that created a glow overhead illuminating chrome appliances and working tables. He opened the refrigerator and practically salivated at the plate of sliced roast beef sitting on the top shelf. In a matter of minutes he had made himself a sandwich stuffed with meat and cheese. He was just about to turn off the lights and return to his room when a set of footsteps echoed on the floor.

Coming toward him was Kacy Judd. She wore a tiny white shirt made of lacy cotton and a pair of cut off jeans showing off long, slender legs. But it wasn't the legs or the top that caught Austin's eye. It was her hair.

It was bright red but Austin was quite certain the color didn't come out of a bottle. It fell to her shoulders in long springy curls that bounced when she walked. When that hair was tucked up beneath a hat it was easy to assume she was a tomboy. But when it hung loose, it made her look all woman. When she saw Austin, she smiled, looking like a cat ready to pounce on a canary.

"Well, lookee who's here. Hungry?" she asked with an arch of one brow.

He felt as guilty as a kid who was caught skipping school by the teacher…which irritated him. This woman wasn't his mother or his teacher or anything to him. And he had a perfect right to get something to eat. After all, the ranch advertised its twenty-four-hour kitchen as a selling point.

"There's nothing like a sandwich at midnight, is there?" she said saucily, then quickly added, "Unless it's a thick juicy steak at dinner." Her grin was devilish.

"All right. You've made your point," he said dryly and started to leave.

"You don't need to eat in your room. I've already seen you."

That comment really annoyed him. "I'm not a man who hides from anything, Ms. Judd."

"No?" She turned her back to him and walked over to the refrigerator. Austin watched her pull out the same plate of beef. "You could have fooled me."

She sat on a stool at the island counter and began to make herself a sandwich. Instead of leaving—which he knew she would interpret as him feeling guilty—he took a stool across from her and plunked his plate down with a thud.

"Just because I don't want to play cowboys with you doesn't mean I'm a coward," he stated in no uncertain terms.

She didn't answer, but gave him a quick glance then continued smearing salad dressing on her bread.

Silence stretched between them until he said, "If this is how you treat your guests I'm surprised you have any sort of reputation left."

This time she was the one who slapped something down on the counter. A knife. It clanged and he saw a spark in her eye that made his heartbeat increase.

"This is not a hotel, Mr. Bennett. It's a ranch. A working ranch and guests who come here do so because they want to be a part of that work. Our job is to provide them with that opportunity, not to cater to self-indulgent, egotistical suits who have little respect for anybody else's property but their own."

By the time she had finished her eyes were flashing, her cheeks red, her chest heaving. It was the heaving chest part that held Austin's attention. There was stress on the buttons of her shirt. And it wasn't only caused by her posture, which was one of agitation. No, that skimpy little shirt of hers was a bit too tight across the bosom. He suspected that it was a deliberate maneuver on her part. He had yet to meet a woman who didn't use her physical attributes to get her own way.

Yup, Ms. Kacy Judd knew exactly what she was doing when she got dressed every morning. If any of the guests were a bit reluctant to get on one of her horses, she could just mosey on over to him, press that knockout of a body next to his, stretch her arms so that those buttons were strained to the max and that little gap would allow the ever-so-tiniest of peeks at the lacy undergarment.

He felt himself growing hard. Damn. She was so good it was working on him. He forced his eyes to her face, but it didn't help. The curve of those cherry lips was just as tantalizing as the peek at her breasts. Maybe he should have gone for the riding lesson after all.

The direction his thoughts were taking made him stop short. What was he thinking letting a cowgirl distract him from the issue—which was his right not to participate in the experiential learning program. For a minute he had almost been ready to concede that she had a point. He reminded himself that he was a paying guest, not a prisoner on the ranch, and he was not a man to endure insults.

He leaned across the counter until his face was only inches from her. "You think I'm self-absorbed because I care about the success of a firm which employs thousands of people? Is that what hard work is to you, Ms. Judd? Self-absorption?"

To his surprise, she didn't back away, but held his gaze and even moved a bit closer to him. "Hard work? You call pencil pushing hard work, Mr. Bennett?" She chuckled sarcastically. "I doubt you'd be able to do a hard day's physical labor if your life depended on it."

He knew she was baiting him. She was trying to get him to prove to her that he could handle the work at the ranch. Against his willpower, every macho nerve screamed for him to prove he could. He was ready to flex his muscles and show her that he was not an office potato but a well-conditioned, athletic, tough guy. Only he knew he wasn't. It had been years since he had been to the gym. With the schedule he worked, there was no time for health clubs.

"I don't need to do your ranch work, Ms. Judd. I make money everyday using this." He tapped his finger on his forehead.

"You think money's the answer to everything, don't you?"

"It's the reason why you're running this ranch as a corporate retreat center," he shot back at her.

He knew he had hit home with that barb. She lowered her eyes as if to compose herself.

"We're just trying to keep doing what we love to do," she answered quietly.

"You can call it anything you want, but you have the same goal as we do in Chicago. To make money. You're entrepreneurs."

"We're ranchers," she stated firmly.

He shrugged. "Whatever."

"We are," she insisted vehemently. "This isn't the city. We're not conjuring up ways to make a fast buck. We want people to understand the connection between the land and life, to show them that what they do in the office has its roots back here on the prairie."

He rolled his eyes. "Spare me the altruism."

She could only shake her head. "How did you become so jaded, Mr. Bennett?"

"I'm not jaded, Ms. Judd. I'm a realist."

"If that's the case then you might want to think about the reality of what you're doing here. Put a little more thought to the morale of your colleagues and a little less about your girlfriend back in Chicago, who by the way has been making a nuisance of herself by leaving countless messages at the switchboard.''

Daphne's persistence annoyed Austin, too, but he wasn't about to let this woman know that. His frustration at not being able to make long-distance phone calls surfaced.

"She wouldn't have to *pester* your switchboard operator if your local phone company had more than one line for long distance. Do you realize how long I've been trying to get a connection to Chicago?''

"Just can't stand being away from your girlfriend, can you?" she said snidely. "What I can't figure out is why you just didn't bring her with you? You two lovebirds could have cuddled poolside while the rest of your employees worked their butts off building fences.''

Gosh, he hated her tone of voice. She had to be the most irritating woman he had ever met. He was just about to retaliate with a rude comment when he realized what was happening. This woman was getting to him. Why was he even standing here arguing with her?

He picked up his sandwich and started to walk toward the door saying, "There's no point in discussing this subject with you. I'll have a word with your superior.''

"You mean my dad?"

It was said with such a smugness Austin knew that she was thinking, *Go ahead. It won't do you any good.* He turned around to look at her. "Why should it matter to you whether or not I take part in the activities?''

She shrugged. "I told you. It doesn't mean a thing to me. But your employees…well, maybe you should ask them how they feel. You might be surprised by what you hear.''

He chucked sardonically. "I've no doubt they want me to be as miserable as they are."

She looked as if he had dealt her a personal blow. "Riding is not misery, Mr. Bennett. It's the most glorious, wonderful...." she trailed off, looking a bit embarrassed by her enthusiasm.

"I'll tell you what. You know the way you feel about riding? That's how I feel about the work I do."

"I don't think so."

"And how would you know? Have you ever experienced the rush of excitement you get from finalizing a deal you know will allow your employees to enjoy the profits of their labor?"

"No, but..."

"Well, until you do, Ms. Judd, I suggest you not try to get me on a horse and I won't ask you to speak at our stockholders' meeting." He thought he had put her in her place but good.

As he walked out of the kitchen he heard her call out to him, "We're rounding up cattle tomorrow at 7:00 a.m. Be there."

KACY SHOULD HAVE known that her talk with Austin Bennett wouldn't produce any results. The following morning he was not with his team members when they went out on the range to round up the cattle. By late afternoon, everyone was tired, dusty and in need of a shower...everyone but Austin, that is.

Dinner was served in the dining room. The atmosphere was a bit subdued, but in a good way. Kacy sat with several members of her team, but noticed that her sister chose to sit next to Austin.

The younger woman flirted shamelessly with the CEO. As hard as Kacy tried not to notice their lighthearted banter, she couldn't keep her eyes off the two of them. It irked Kacy that Suzy was being so friendly to the guy when he was completely ignoring the efforts of everyone involved with the program. She wanted everyone at the ranch to shun the man.

Although there was no planned activity for that evening, one of the assignments was to fill out a questionnaire which was a leadership pretest. Kacy didn't expect Austin to answer any questions. While everyone else sat with pencil and paper in hand, he disappeared. She guessed he had gone back to his room, since it was where he spent most of his time. Kacy sat in the lounge watching as one by the one the guests finished with the test and handed her their papers. When she had collected everyone's but Austin's, she decided to pay him a visit.

At first she thought he wasn't in his room, for no one answered her knock. However, as she was about to leave, the door opened. Standing with only a towel around his waist, his hair dripping with water, he looked as surprised as she felt.

The sight of his bare chest had her shifting from one foot to the other. Of their own volition, her eyes traveled down the length of torso, following the fuzzy light trail of hair extending from his belly button down to... She jerked her eyes upward. What was she thinking? Looking down as if she were curious about what was beneath the towel.

She must have stood there speechless for several seconds because he said a bit impatiently, "Well?"

She waved the stack of papers in the air. "I need yours."

"My what? I take it it's not an evaluation form otherwise you wouldn't be asking me for it," he drawled.

"It's called a pretest. You fill it out this evening and

we go over the answers tomorrow. It's a way for you to assess what you know about leadership.'' He stood there giving her a blank look. "I don't have yours."

"Because I didn't do it." His voice was flat and disinterested.

"I know." He smelled like soap and something else…maybe a designer shaving cream. It was a combination that had the awareness hairs prickling on Kacy's skin.

"So?"

"So would you please get yours done?"

He sighed. "I really don't have the time."

"It's a simple little exercise that we'll be using tomorrow at the meeting. It'll take you fifteen minutes max."

He shoved his hands to his hips. "What's the point?"

"The point is we're going to use them tomorrow. You can at least attend a meeting that's held by the pool, can't you?"

Again he sighed. "Where is this paper?"

"They were passed out at dinner."

"I must have left it in the dining room."

"No problem. I have an extra." She flipped through the stack only to discover she didn't have an extra. "I guess I don't have one. I'll tell you what. I'll read you the questions and you can give me your answers. I'll mark them on a blank sheet of paper and transfer them to a form when I get back to the office."

"You want to come in?" He looked as skeptical as she felt.

"You can get dressed first."

"I wasn't getting dressed. I was going to bed."

Which meant he probably slept naked, Kacy thought.

She could feel the roots of her hair blushing. She opened her mouth to speak but nothing came out.

He stepped aside and motioned for her to enter.

She hesitated until he said, "You can leave the door open if it makes you feel better."

"Don't flatter yourself," she muttered as she stepped inside.

He reached for a hanger from the closet. "If you'll excuse me a minute, I'll get dressed." Then he disappeared into the bathroom.

At the sound of a hair dryer, Kacy decided she'd better take a seat at the round table that was littered with papers. Besides a laptop, there was a fax machine, a power surge strip, a printer and a half-eaten bag of horehound drops.

"So much for unplugging," she murmured to herself. Just then the phone rang. She waited for Austin to come out of the bathroom, but he didn't. Thinking the sound of his hair dryer probably prohibited him from hearing the ringing of the phone, she decided to answer it.

"Who is this?" the woman's voice on the other end demanded upon hearing Kacy's voice.

"To whom do you wish to speak?" Kacy responded primly.

"Where's Austin?"

The image of a sultry brunette wearing a slinky negligee flashed in Kacy's mind. It was that kind of voice. "He can't come to the phone right now," she answered honestly. "Would you like to leave a message?"

"Who is this?" an angry voice demanded.

"Who is this?" Kacy countered.

"This is Daphne Delattre, who just so happens to be Austin's fiancée," she hissed.

"This is Kacy Judd, the woman who just so happens

to be in his room." Kacy should have felt ashamed, but she didn't.

"Well, as soon as he can come to the phone, I expect him to call me."

And before Kacy could say another word, the woman hung up. "And it was nice talking to you, too," she said to the receiver before placing it back on the cradle. "I'd say you two deserve each other."

A few minutes later when Austin appeared, Kacy gave him the message. "Your *fiancée* called."

"I don't have a fiancée," he replied curtly.

Kacy shrugged. "Well, the woman who called here a few minutes ago seemed to think you did."

He exhaled a long sigh. "She must have dialed the wrong room."

"You don't know a Daphne Delattre?"

"Yes, but she's not my fiancée."

"Oh." It was said with such innocence he could take it any way he wanted. She thought he might offer some explanation, but he didn't. After what she had heard in the airport and then in the pickup on the way to the ranch, it came as no surprise to Kacy that Austin Bennett wanted no strings attached to him.

Kacy could almost feel sorry for the woman. Almost. As persistent as this Daphne sounded, the battle ahead of her was insurmountable if she thought she could get this man to commit to a trip down the wedding aisle.

"Can we get these questions out of the way?" he asked impatiently.

"Of course." She motioned with her arm. "Take a seat and we'll get right to it."

As she sat across from him she couldn't help but notice that he smelled even better than he had when soap had been his only perfume. He had slipped into a pair of shorts which revealed the thick muscles of his thighs and a blue shirt that emphasized his broad shoulders. She forced her attention to the stack of papers in front of her.

"I want you to rate on a scale of one to ten the following statements," she began. "One is low and ten is very high."

As she read off the questions he didn't pause to contemplate his answers, but rattled them off, one after another. To Kacy's surprise, each of his answers was a ten. When she was finished, she went over several of the questions a second time.

"You know how to motivate people."

"Yes."

"You're good at talking to groups and communicating your wishes?"

"Yes.

"You think others would rate you as a ten as a leader?"

"Yes."

She could have gone right down the list and he would have answered the same way. "I'm supposed to ask you which three topics you'd like to learn more about, but it's obvious from your answers that you have all the answers." She looked then into his blue eyes. It was a mistake. They were the same color as the polo shirt he wore.

"No, it just means I don't need to play games." Those blue eyes pinned hers with an intensity that caused her hands to tremble.

"This isn't a game." She took a deep breath to control her frustration. Then she picked up the stack of papers and got up to go. "Thank you for your time. I'll add your results to the rest of the group and see you tomorrow at the leadership seminar."

He followed her to the door. "I thought we just determined that I don't need the seminar."

She paused in the open doorway to turn and face him. "Would it be so difficult for you to participate in *one* workshop?"

He let out a huge sigh, as if he were making a supreme sacrifice. "Where's it at?"

"If it's not raining it'll be outside at the pool."

"I'll think about it." He was about to close the door when she noticed he didn't have a Do Not Disturb door hanger. Every guest upon their arrival had been given the paper hanger to use in case they didn't want to be woken up in the middle of the night to witness the birthing of a colt. On her walk down the hallway, Kacy had noticed several of them in place. Austin's wasn't.

"Is there anything else, Ms. Judd?" he asked.

She debated for a couple of seconds whether or not she should tell him. "Ah, no. That's it for tonight."

"Very well. Goodnight." He dismissed her as if she were an employee.

"Goodnight, Mr. Bennett," she said cheerfully, pausing to see if he would slip the door hanger in place. He didn't.

She smiled as she walked away. Her pregnant mare, Beauty Mark, had been dripping milk for the past two days—which meant she was close to having that foal. With any luck, it would be tonight.

Chapter Four

It was the ringing of the telephone that woke Austin. A glance at the digital clock told him it was three fifty-seven. Still dark. Still night. Still time to be sleeping. Groggily he reached for the phone.

"This better be good," he growled into the receiver.

"Beauty Mark's in labor. You need to hurry if you don't want to miss it." The voice was eager, animated. A direct contrast to the way Austin was feeling.

"What?" he demanded angrily.

"The mare. She's ready to foal."

"So why are you calling me?"

"Because your name is on the list. You'd better hurry, Mr. Bennett. The van's going to leave in ten minutes."

Austin slammed the receiver down. He plopped his head back on the bed and groaned. The birth of a colt? What list? He had signed up for nothing. Had that Judd woman deliberately added his name so that she would interrupt his sleep?

Thinking that had to be the case, he jumped out of bed and quickly dressed. If she thought she could get away with a prank like this, she was sorely mistaken. In less than five minutes he was marching toward the lobby.

"Hey, Mr. Bennett! This is a surprise," Ed Patterson,

one of the district sales managers, greeted him in the hallway. "I didn't expect you'd be getting up in the middle of the night to do anything." Seeing the thunderous look on his boss's face, he quickly added, "That didn't come out the way I meant it. What I wanted to say is I think it's great that you finally decided to join us. We thought maybe you were just here to spy on us."

It was said with a chuckle, but Austin knew that it probably wasn't far from the truth. Before he could set the record straight, however, they were joined by several other Bennett employees making their way toward the front door. All looked as if they'd pulled on their clothes in a hurry. All appeared to have something to say about his appearance.

"Mr. Bennett got up for this?"

"Hey, it's about time you joined us, boss."

"Better late than never."

Austin almost said that it was *never,* not late, but something stopped him. Maybe it was their enthusiasm. They sounded like a bunch of young kids on their way to see the Cubs play. Austin had to practically run to keep up with them as they hurried toward the parking lot.

Like the others, he climbed into the van and took a seat in the back. Mark Judd slid behind the wheel and drove them the short distance, stopping outside a smaller barn than the one Austin had seen at the Triple J. Outside was the orange pickup which Austin knew meant that Kacy was inside.

When he entered the barn he could see that the horses who used these stalls were someone's pride and joy. Blue ribbons lined the walls and green velvet draped the gates. A pillow on a cot indicated it wasn't uncommon for a human to sleep here if necessary.

Leaning against the door on one of the stalls was Kacy Judd, concern lining her face. She wore a white blouse and a pair of jeans, her hair a mass of untamed curls as if she, too, had been awakened from her sleep.

When she noticed Austin, she looked surprised to see him. He wasn't fooled. He didn't doubt for a moment that she had added his name to the list of guests who wanted to see the foaling.

She waved the group closer. Austin went and stood directly behind her, ready to give her a piece of his mind. Up close he could smell a tangy, tropical scent and once again he noticed that her buttons didn't hold the fronts of her blouse together very well.

"I need to speak to you in private," he told her, trying to ignore the creamy white skin peeking through the openings of her shirt.

"You'll have to wait until after Beauty Mark has foaled," she told him, then stepped up onto a bale of hay to address the group. "You're just in time. We expect the new baby to arrive any minute now."

"Don't you need to call a vet?" one of the men asked.

"Not unless she has trouble. She's been through this before and she's never had any problems, so we're assuming she'll do just fine with this baby."

"Shouldn't someone be in there with her?" another guest inquired.

"Oh no," Kacy quickly shot back. "You don't want to be in a stall when a horse is foaling unless she's in trouble and needs help." She went on to explain what was going to happen, answering questions from the small group gathered around her.

Suddenly someone announced, "Look! It's coming!"

Austin watched as the foal was delivered forefeet first,

its head tucked between the hoofs. A collective sigh could be heard as the tiny horse emerged.

"Look!" Kacy grabbed the first arm she could reach, which just happened to be Austin's. "Isn't she beautiful?" When she turned and noticed whose arm it was that she had grabbed, she released it, looking a bit embarrassed by her display of emotion.

Once more the guests bombarded her with questions, which she patiently answered. While everyone else watched the foal and mare, Austin watched Kacy. The way she spoke with her hands. The way she kept one eye on the horse and mare yet gave her attention to the guests. The way her slender body moved with the grace of a dancer.

Seeing her with the horses made him realize that she truly was a cowgirl, not just someone trying to sell a ranch retreat to the corporate world. As he watched her he forgot all the harsh words he had planned to say to her. He forgot that it was four in the morning, that he didn't want any part of the Triple J experience.

What he wanted was for Kacy to give him the same kind of attention she was giving the others. He wanted her to call him Austin, just as she was calling the other guests by their first names. But mostly he wanted that smile to be cast in his direction.

Only it wasn't. She looked at everyone but him.

When the foal managed to stand on wobbly legs, a round of applause acknowledged the feat. Kacy fielded another round of questions as they watched in amusement as the newborn tottered on unsteady legs. Smiles accompanied sounds of understanding as the foal nudged various parts of her mother's body.

"She's hungry," was the unanimous conclusion.

Finally Mark Judd announced he'd be taking everyone

back to the lodge. One by one the spectators left, but Austin stuck around, determined to speak to Kacy.

When they were the only two left in the barn, she looked at him and said, "I didn't expect to see you here."

"Didn't you?"

"No. Is there a reason why I should have?"

He shrugged. "I just thought maybe you knew how my name ended up on the list of people who requested to be called at four o'clock to watch a mare give birth."

"We automatically assume everyone wants to be notified unless they hang the Do Not Disturb sign on their doorknobs." She gave him the most innocent look he had ever seen on a woman's face. "You must not have hung your sign."

"And that's why I was called?"

"Umm-hmm. What's wrong, Mr. Bennett? Did you think I had put your name on the list to punish you for not riding today?"

He knew she knew that's exactly what he had thought. "How come I wasn't told about this doorknob thing?"

"Maybe because you weren't at the orientation meeting," she answered.

He looked for the usual smug twinkle in her eye, but it wasn't there.

"It was also in the packet of information I gave you when you arrived," she added, again without any hint of criticism.

The only part of that packet he had looked at had been the riding instructions. He had thought she had arranged for him to be awakened to get even with him for not attending the riding lessons when all along it had been his own fault. Humble pie gathered in his mouth.

"What? Nothing to say, Mr. Bennett?" she asked, her eyebrow lifting.

The twinkle in her eye was back. It would have been easy to get into another verbal sparring match with her, but he didn't want to.

He glanced over at the filly and said, "I've never seen a horse foal before."

"And what did you think?" she asked.

Before he could answer Dusty interrupted. "Kacy, if we're going to go in, we should do it now."

"Go in?" Austin's brows drew together. "I thought you said it was dangerous to go in a stall with a mare and her foal."

"It is," she said simply, then opened the gate. Carefully, the two of them approached the mare and foal.

"Easy does it, girl," Dusty spoke softly, gently easing his hands around Beauty Mark's halter. While he held onto the mare, Kacy carefully put her hands on the foal.

Beauty Mark whinnied and Austin said, "I don't think you should be doing that."

It was Dusty who answered, "Don't worry, Mr. Bennett. Kacy knows what she's doing."

Austin watched as she tended to the newborn with gentle hands. When she had finished with the foal, she turned her attention to Beauty Mark. "Good job, girl. I am so proud of you. Thanks for letting me touch your little one," she cooed in the horse's ear.

Austin watched Kacy give the mare a bucket of water while Dusty removed the dirty bedding from the stall. When they had finished, she pushed open the rolling gate and carefully stepped out of the stall.

"What happens tomorrow?" Austin asked.

"There's a trail ride after the leadership seminar, then the afternoon is free," she replied.

"No, I mean with the horses?" He nodded toward the newborn.

"Oh. We'll put them out, but they'll have to be alone for several days. Otherwise, the other mares will go after the foal. If you want you can get a look at how they're doing tomorrow afternoon. Mark's going to bring a vanload of people over." She tried to hide a yawn but was unsuccessful.

"Have you been up all night?" Austin asked.

"Just since two. Dusty and I took turns watching her." She eyed him suspiciously. "Why are you looking at me like that?"

"Like what?"

"Do I have muck on my face or something?" She ran her forearm across her forehead in a self-conscious manner.

"No, you don't have anything on your face," he answered, suddenly aware that as irritating as Kacy Judd could be at times, he liked being with her.

He had come out to the barn expecting to tell her off. Instead he was standing here a bit mesmerized by her prettiness. For she was pretty, especially with her red curls springing loose around her face. And whether or not it was because she was tired, there was vulnerability in her face that appealed to him. Actually, everything about her appealed to him.

He couldn't, however, tell her that. So he said, "I was just thinking how different you look when you don't wear your hat."

Automatically her hand grabbed the untamed red curls, bunching them together as she pushed them away from her face. "My hat doesn't just keep the rain from my face. It hides this mop of mine."

"You have beautiful hair. You shouldn't hide it." He

didn't mean for it to come out as if he were making a pass at her, but that's exactly what happened.

She stiffened. "I don't hide it," she said, obviously uncomfortable with the compliment. "It's easier to work if I don't have to worry about it getting in the way."

They were interrupted again by Dusty who said, "They should be all right till morning."

Kacy gave her brother a quick hug. "Thanks for watching her for me." She turned once more toward the foal and said, "She is a beauty, isn't she?"

The smile that lit her face did funny things to Austin's insides.

Dusty agreed, then turned to Austin. "It's late. We'd better get out of here so Kacy can get to bed. I just have to check on another mare, then I can give you a ride back to the lodge. I'll meet you in say…five minutes?"

Austin nodded, then turned to Kacy. "Are you going to sleep out here?"

She shoved her hands to her hips. "Now why should it concern you where I sleep, Mr. Bennett?"

The antagonism was back between them and he wasn't sure why. So much for anything changing between them tonight. "Forget I asked," he said irritably and walked away without so much as a glance back at Kacy.

It probably was just as well. She didn't want his attention and he knew he would be wise to squash any thoughts of flirting with a cowgirl. As he headed back to the lodge he decided that Kacy Judd was not going to distract him from the work that needed to be done. No matter how pretty she was.

KACY MADE SURE she wasn't at the same breakfast table as Austin Bennett. She hadn't liked the way his eyes had looked at her last night or the tone of voice he had used when he had told her she had beautiful hair. She didn't want a man who bothered her so much taking an interest in anything she did. She attacked her pancakes with a vengeance, angry with herself for even thinking about the man at all.

The only thing last night had shown her was that Mr. Austin Bennett was no different than any of the other city men she had known. She hadn't missed the way his eyes had watched her climb up onto the hay bale, watched every little move she made. Just the thought of those blue eyes on her rear end sent a little tremor through her—which only increased her annoyance with the man.

After last night she was glad that he wasn't participating in any of the activities. At least she wouldn't have to put up with those sexy blue eyes looking at her as though she were a carrot being dangled in front of a horse. He didn't realize what a favor he was doing for her by not joining in the group's activities.

That's why she was caught completely off guard when he walked into the dining room wearing a pair of jeans, a long-sleeved western shirt and a shiny new pair of boots.

"Suzy, why is Mr. Bennett dressed like that?" she asked her sister.

"I had a message from him first thing this morning asking if I could open the shop for him," the younger woman answered. "He's going riding."

"What do you mean he's going riding?" Kacy almost choked on her pancakes.

"That *is* why people come here," Suzy pointed out with a chuckle. "He says he would have gone before now but he's been working on some special project for his work that kept him from joining the others.''

"Yeah, right," Kacy drawled sarcastically.

"I don't know why you don't like him. We don't get many single men here and when they do come, they don't look like that. He's gorgeous," Suzy gushed as if she were sixteen instead of twenty-two.

"He has a fiancée," Kacy said stiffly.

Suzy frowned. "Not the pesky Daphne?"

"She's keeping close tabs on her man."

"I don't blame her. I would, too, if I had a guy who looked like that," Suzy said dreamily, a forkful of grapefruit poised in midair.

Kacy had to admit that he was indeed gorgeous. And to make matters worse, he looked good in western wear. She wanted him to look like a fish out of water, not as though he could be the poster boy for denim jeans.

"You really think he's riding today?" Out of the corner of her eye Kacy watched him sit down beside a couple of his team members.

"Why else would he buy boots?" Suzy asked. "I don't think it was to look like everyone else, do you?"

No, it definitely wasn't Mr. Bennett's style to do anything to fit in. He was a man who marched to the beat of his own drum. The question was why did he now have the urge to ride?

"I wonder if he's even been on a horse," Kacy mused aloud.

"Just because he lives in Chicago doesn't mean he can't ride."

She made a disgruntled sound of disagreement. "He'll slow the rest of us down. He should have been at the riding lesson the very first session."

"Well, he wasn't, and you know what Dad says."

"I know. Do whatever we can to accommodate the guests." She tossed her napkin on her plate and gathered her things. "That's easier said than done."

"If I didn't have to work the front desk, I'd go out with you," Suzy offered.

Having her younger sister drooling over Austin Bennett was not what Kacy needed. "It's all right. I'll manage."

"Have fun," Suzy called out as Kacy carried her dishes to the kitchen.

Fun was not a possibility as far as Kacy was concerned.

Just as she was leaving the dining room, Austin caught up with her.

"I'm ready for that riding lesson now," he said in a tone she suspected he used often with his employees. It reeked of "me boss, you slave."

She stopped in her tracks and folded her arms across her chest. "We're leaving on a ride as soon as the leadership seminar is over."

"Yes. That's why I need the lesson. Since I passed your test, I'll skip the seminar. Thirty minutes should be enough time to get me up on a horse." When she shot him a dubious look he gave her a smile that could have charmed a snake. "I'm a fast learner."

As far as she was concerned, that charming smile only added insult to injury. She found his arrogance offensive. He assumed that he was entitled to the lesson without giving a second thought to whether or not it might be an inconvenience for her.

"You're missing the point. I gave riding lessons earlier this week." She used the tone she had perfected while living in New York—the one she jokingly referred to as her take-no-crap voice.

"Are you saying you won't teach me?" he asked in a dangerously calm voice.

She tried to ignore her father's words, but they echoed in her ears like raindrops on a metal roof. "We're counting on you, Kacy, to make sure we maintain a reputation of doing whatever is necessary to see that our guests are satisfied." Until this week, it hadn't been a problem.

"Of course I'll teach you," she conceded. "Only today's ride is a long one. Even if I give you the basic lesson, you're going to get sore if you try to keep up with the others who've been on horses since Monday. Riding is a physical exertion."

"I'm not afraid of a little exercise." Challenge lit his eyes. "So what do you say? Do I get the lesson I've paid for?"

"Sure. Let's go get you a horse." As she started toward the door she muttered under her breath, "It's your backside."

"I HOPE YOU READ the information in your packet on riding," Kacy said as she led a chestnut quarter horse into the corral.

"As a matter of fact, I did," he told her, leaning against the fence. "Never surprise a horse. Lead with caution. Watch where you're going."

She tried not to be impressed as he rattled off the safety rules she had provided each of the guests, but the truth was, he was one of only a few who had done his homework. Of course he had had several more days than the others to do that homework. Still, it made her job easier.

"Good. It helps to be prepared." She brought the horse closer to him. "This is Marshmallow. She's a twelve-year-old who's aptly named. She's as gentle as they come.''

She could tell by the look on his face that he wasn't convinced.

''I wouldn't put a beginner on a difficult horse,'' she assured him.

''Not even guests who don't follow the rules?'' He grinned slightly and she couldn't prevent the answering smile that creased her lips.

''You can relax, Mr. Bennett.''

''I am relaxed. And why don't you call me Austin, Kacy.'' The way he said her name sent a shiver through her. It was almost a caress and so very different from the usual sarcasm he used.

''All right, Austin, why don't you come get acquainted with Marshmallow?'' She motioned for him to touch the horse. ''Let him smell you. Watch his eyes and ears. If his ears are relaxed, you can relax.''

He followed her lead, brushing a hand down the animal's neck and muttering words of affection. As Kacy expected, Marshmallow warmed to him immediately. If there was one given, it was that Marshmallow was a sucker for praise, and Austin laid it on thick. He talked to the horse as if she were a woman he wanted to bed.

The thought sent another shiver through Kacy. Again, she noticed a sexual tension in the air. It was becoming a regular thing when she was around Austin Bennett.

''All right. Let's get started.'' She took a deep breath and asked, ''Have you ever been on a horse?''

''Once when I was kid. It went around in a circle.'' He gave her a devilish grin and she felt her heart flip-flop.

''Well, Marshmallow isn't going to take you in circles.''

Kacy discovered Austin to be a good student, listening intently and paying close attention to details. For someone whose only experience had been sitting astride a pony at a carnival, he did remarkably well and appeared to be a natural in the saddle.

That didn't please Kacy at all. It would have been much easier to dislike the man if he had hated her horses. And she didn't want him to be a part of a world she loved dearly. She could feel herself softening toward him and she didn't want to have any feelings for Austin Bennett except indifference.

"Is this the horse I'll be riding?" he asked when it was time to join the others.

"You can have Marshmallow for today."

"And what about tomorrow?"

"You've decided to finish the course?"

"Don't look so unhappy about it," he chastised.

"I'm not unhappy," she lied. "Your employees need you to take part in the activities. It's just too bad you missed the first half of the course. It's not going to be easy catching up."

"Let me worry about that," he said in a condescending tone that once more reminded her that he was the one in control.

As he started to walk away she called out to him, "You're going to need a hat. The sun is relentless this time of the year."

"Let me guess. I can buy one in the guest shop."

"Any hat will do," she retorted. "You might want to consider only doing part of the ride today. I could probably find someone to ride back with you."

"You don't need to worry about me, Kacy. I can handle it."

"All right. If that's the way you want it."

"It is," he said confidently.

Kacy simply shrugged. Before they went to join the others, her final words to him were "Don't say I didn't warn you."

As much as Austin hated to admit it, he wanted to go on the trail ride. The more he saw of Kacy Judd, the more interested he became in taking part in the activities she led. Ever since he had seen her red curls springing about in sexy disarray, she had been under his skin. She was like a bug bite. She didn't belong under his skin, but she was there, drawing more of his attention than he could afford to spare.

His ego was to blame. Because she was such an independent, feisty little thing, he had this urge to prove himself to her. It wasn't that he needed to show her that he could ride. He just wanted to let her know that she couldn't intimidate him into *not* riding, which is what she had been trying to do ever since that first day when he wouldn't take part in the group activities.

It was a battle of wills that had been started the minute she had picked him up at the airport. Until today, she had won the battle. But now he was going to turn the tables.

There was no doubt in Austin's mind when he climbed aboard Marshmallow that Kacy didn't want him riding out with the team. He smiled to himself. It was that very fact that was going to make the long ride worth any discomfort he might experience.

Or so he thought.

He wasn't sure how many miles they rode that morning, but when they finally returned to the Triple J, Austin knew it had been too many. Despite the fact that he was sore all over, he refused to let Kacy see even so much as a grimace on his face.

If he could have disappeared into his room, he would have been all right. But before that could happen, the horses needed to be groomed and put away. As he lifted the saddle from Marshmallow's back, he couldn't hide the discomfort in his limbs.

"Are you all right, Mr. Bennett?" she asked. "You look as if you're having trouble bending over." He could see she could barely hide her pleasure at the thought.

"I'm fine," he lied.

"You sure?"

Austin used every bit of strength he had to pretend he was without an ache in his body. "Yes, I'm sure."

She just shrugged and put her horse away. As Austin dragged his weary body back to the lodge, Ed Patterson caught up with him.

"I know how you feel, boss. The first day my knees were killing me after riding."

Austin glanced over his shoulder to make sure Kacy wasn't within earshot. "My feet feel numb."

"I bet your rear end is sore, too, isn't it?"

"I don't think there's a part of me that doesn't ache. I know where I'm spending the rest of the day."

Ed gave him a knowing grin. "The Jacuzzi."

"You got it."

"I was thinking about doing the same thing. If we're going to be sleeping outside tonight I figure I'd better enjoy the comfort of the lodge this afternoon."

Austin frowned. "We're sleeping outside?"

He chuckled. "Didn't they give you a schedule?" Concluding that his boss had been kept in the dark, he continued, "We're riding out to some creek to rough it together." He rubbed his jaw thoughtfully. "I don't know. I've never slept on the ground and I'm not sure I want to. I mean, what if there are snakes around here?''

Austin didn't want to sleep on the ground and it had nothing to do with snakes, but the fact that every muscle in his body screamed for a feather bed.

"I guess that's the whole point of the exercise, though,'' Ed remarked. ''To prove to yourself that you can do more than you ever thought you were capable of doing. And it'll help us build trust—you know, having to rely on each other in the middle of nowhere.''

Austin was just about to say he wasn't going to go along on the camp out when Ed added, ''Kacy told us you've decided to finish the course and I have to tell you, that's really good news to the rest of us. I mean, no offense, boss, but we've been sweating our butts off out there while you were back at the pool and…'' he trailed off uneasily. ''Well, you know.''

"It was work keeping me from joining you, Ed,'' Austin told him, feeling a bit uncomfortable with the half truth. ''I've taken care of it so I can finish up the program with the rest of you.''

"That's great. It'll be good to have you there.'' He gave him a mock salute and headed for his room, leaving Austin with the grim knowledge that if he wanted his employees' respect, he had no choice but to participate in the camp out.

When he got back to his room the message light on his phone was blinking. Daphne. Who else would be calling him here? He ignored it and stripped out of his clothes, leaving a trail to the bath where he wasted no time running the water for the Whirlpool tub.

As he sank down into the swirling water, he closed his eyes and wondered how he was going to get back up on Marshmallow in only a few hours time. He supposed he could tell everyone an unexpected business deal had cropped up that needed his attention.

If he did, he knew exactly what would happen. Kacy would smile that smug grin, the one that made him want to grab her and kiss her senseless. She was probably just waiting for him to admit defeat. He wasn't going to do it. He wouldn't give her the satisfaction. Nor would he disappoint his employees.

Whether he could feel his feet or not, he was going to go on that overnight adventure. And as for his legs…already the therapeutic action of the water had already eased some of the pain.

Later, as he towel-dried limbs still throbbing with pain, he knew he had another option. The ranch had a masseuse on staff.

With a towel wrapped around his waist, he limped over to the desk. In the leather-bound folder listing guest services he found the number. He glanced at the clock radio. If he were lucky he could get an appointment before the group rode out that evening. He picked up the phone and dialed the extension printed on the parchment paper.

"Health club," a man's voice traveled through the wires.

"Ah, yes, this is Austin Bennett. Would it be possible to get a massage within the next hour or so?"

"Let me check."

While Austin waited he heard the man call out, "Hey Kacy. Can you squeeze a massage in before you head out this evening?"

Kacy? Austin nearly slammed the receiver down. The woman was a masseuse? Good grief. The last woman he wanted working on his aching muscles was Kacy Judd.

There was a long silence with muffled sounds in the

background. Austin suspected that Kacy had learned who it was requesting the massage and was arguing with her brother. Finally, the man returned to the phone.

"I'm sorry, Mr. Bennett, but it's not going to work out today. Would you like to schedule an appointment for tomorrow?"

"No!" He practically shouted into the phone, then recovered himself. "No, it's all right. I'm fine. I just thought if the timing would work..." he trailed off feeling ridiculous. He could just imagine Kacy at the health club smirking because he was suffering.

Well, he would show her. Tonight. He was not a city slicker who couldn't stand a little pain. She'd see. One way or the other, he would take care of that smug grin. Desire stirred in his loins at the thought. Now *every* part of his body ached.

Chapter Five

Austin had only been camping once—the summer he went to Montana to visit his cousins. It had not been the most memorable experience of his life. Four boys in a tent in the mountains. All he could remember was that the ground was hard and his bedroll didn't keep out the cold.

He wondered if this experience would be much different. A sleeping bag should keep him warm, but the ground would probably be just as hard. He thought about bringing a pillow. Not for his head, but for his rear so that when he sat in the saddle he'd have a cushion. He could only imagine what the ''I told you so'' cowgirl would have to say about that. The Whirlpool had eased some of the aches and pains, but the thought of getting back in the saddle was sheer torture.

A rap on the door was followed by a man's voice calling out, ''Party's leaving in fifteen minutes.''

He was tempted to shout back, ''Don't wait for me,'' but he couldn't. He had told everybody he was going along and if there was one thing everyone knew about Austin Bennett, it was that once he said he would do something, he did it.

With a grimace he pulled on the cowboy boots. All

he was allowed to bring was the clothing on his back plus whatever he could fit in the saddlebag or his pockets. They were roughing it. Austin shook his head at the thought of not having a change of clothes.

Even though the temperature had climbed well into the eighties that afternoon, he knew the night would be cool. Over his western shirt he slipped on his windbreaker. He stuck his cellular phone in his pocket and figured he could put his palmtop in his saddlebag. Maybe he couldn't bring his laptop, but he wasn't going to be stuck out on the prairie with nothing to do. Before he walked out the door, he made sure he had his pen size flashlight as well.

As the parade of horses and riders left the Triple J, the sun was making its descent toward the horizon. They hadn't traveled far when the group was divided into three sections with a member of the Triple J taking charge of each segment. Once more Austin was assigned to Kacy's team. She didn't look any more pleased about it than he did.

The six members of the team headed for a smattering of trees which looked lost and forlorn in the distance. Kacy Judd led the procession, seldom looking in Austin's direction. He was glad. He was doing everything he possibly could to pretend that it wasn't killing him to sit in the saddle, but the truth was it took every bit of his willpower not to get off the horse and beg someone to send for the Triple J van to come get him and take him back to the lodge.

Finally they stopped in front of a dilapidated-looking cabin that had a small corral with a lean-to nearby. He wondered if he had been brought here because it was payback time?

Austin shook himself mentally. The woman truly was

getting under his skin. First he had thought she looked unhappy to have him on her team, now he was accusing her of deliberately trying to make him suffer. What was it about her that made him lose his perspective? Besides her sexy swagger, that is.

"Here's where we'll camp for the night," she said as she dismounted. "As you can see there's a cabin, but we won't use it unless the weather turns bad. Besides, it has nothing we don't have out here except for a roof." Amusement twinkled in her eyes.

He watched her call out instructions, taking control of the situation with an authority that came as no surprise to him. She was a woman accustomed to giving orders. It should have put him off. If there was one thing he didn't like in women it was the constant need to tell some man what to do.

Yet this woman was different from any he had ever known. Her self-confidence wasn't derived from how she looked, but rather what she could do. It was refreshing to meet a woman who took more pride in what she accomplished than in her appearance. He had a pretty good idea that if a man were to kiss her he wouldn't have to worry about messing up her hair or makeup.

"Mr. Bennett, you're not moving. Did you hear what I said?"

Actually, he hadn't. He had been lost in his thoughts, watching the way her hips swayed as she moved back and forth between the horses. Well worn denim revealed tight buns and thighs. She wore a long-sleeved purple shirt with white fringe. With her fancy stitched boots and her straw hat she looked as though she could be on the stage of the Grand Ole Opry.

"This is a team effort, Mr. Bennett. We need you to

pull your share of the work," she said in no uncertain terms.

"My share being what, Ms. Judd?" he asked.

"We need to make a fire pit. You're in charge of finding the rocks."

He looked around. "And where might I find rocks out here?"

"There's a creek on the other side of those trees," she told him, nodding toward the copse of green to their right. "Take your partner with you."

"My partner?"

"Caroline."

He glanced at the two women in his group. Both looked familiar, but he didn't remember either one's name.

Kacy lowered her voice as she said, "If you had been with us from day one you would know who she was. Actually, you should know anyway. She's *your* employee."

He knew she was right. He should have at least made an effort to talk to each of the Bennett employees. What he didn't need, however, was for this slip of a cowgirl to point out his shortcomings as a boss.

Annoyed, he said, "Look, why don't I just get the rocks myself."

"Because this is supposed to be a team effort," she said dryly. "Caroline's the one wearing the red shirt. The other one is Sharon." Then she added in an irritating whisper, "She works for you, too."

Austin could have recited statistics on each of the women's work performances, but the truth of the matter was he wouldn't have been able to identify either one without the help of Kacy. Personnel relations had never been his strong suit. Actually, it wasn't a suit at all. If he didn't work directly with an employee, he didn't see much purpose in getting to know the person. After all, his work was to make money for the company, not make small talk with its employees.

"How big a pit do you want?" he asked, refusing to be baited by her.

With the toe of her boot she traced a circle in the sand. "It's best to be quick. Dusk appears to linger forever out here, but it'll soon be dark."

Austin would have preferred to gather the rocks without the help of Caroline, but Kacy was determined that every task would be done in pairs.

As the two of them headed for the creek, Caroline said, "You look like you feel the way I felt on my first day here."

"Riding doesn't look like it should create so many aches in so many places, does it?" he said with a grimace.

"No, but this is a totally different kind of work than what we're used to."

"I bet you never expected hauling rocks would be part of your job when you were hired, did you?" he asked, placing a gray boulder along the outline Kacy had drawn.

"This isn't your typical business conference," she admitted as she dusted her hands on the legs of her jeans.

"Have you found it useful?"

"Sort of."

"You don't sound convinced."

"I'm not much of an outdoor person and personally, I'm not sure whether what we're doing will transfer to our jobs once we're back in New York. What do you think, sir?"

Austin didn't want anyone to call him sir. It made him feel as if he didn't belong with the group.

"Why don't you call me Austin, Caroline? I'm supposed to be your partner, not your boss."

"You don't mind?"

"No, why should I?"

"Because it's rather well known that you..." she broke off uneasily.

"That I what?" he prodded.

"That you would rather keep things on a more formal basis."

He grinned. "It's rather hard to be formal when one's wearing a cowboy hat and boots."

She smiled back at him. "That's true. So. Do you really think what we're doing is going to help us sell furniture?"

He could tell by her tone of voice she didn't think it would. Instead of expressing his own doubts, he simply said, "I guess that remains to be seen, doesn't it?"

By the time they had retrieved enough rocks to make the fire pit, Caroline's disposition was in the same state as Austin's muscles. Tired. As she slapped the dirt from her hands she said, "I hope this means we don't have to do clean up after everyone's eaten."

While they had been hauling the rocks, the others had been gathering kindling and pumping water at the well. To be fair to Kacy, Austin knew that the labor had been divided equally between the members of the group.

If he had expected that there would be a cook to prepare their supper, he was wrong. Seeing the chuck wagon pull in, Austin could see the relief on the faces of his employees. However, the cook didn't stay. As soon as he had dropped off the food and bedding, he had gone on to the next site. The six of them were alone except for the horses.

They ate beans and stew off tin plates and drank coffee cooked with eggshells in a kettle over the open flame. After the last cup was gone, they washed the dishes in a tub Kacy referred to as "the wreck pan" with water that had been heated over the fire. As darkness settled around them, they sat around the campfire telling stories. At least the others told stories. Austin listened.

And watched Kacy. In the firelight her face took on a glow that made him want to move closer to her. He didn't. After the storytelling came the singing. It didn't matter that they had no music, Kacy clapped her hands in rhythm and led them in songs which were easy enough to pick up after hearing a few lines repeated.

Then she announced, "All right. It's time for the last activity for tonight. Everyone on your feet and make a circle."

Getting up was not something Austin wanted to do. His feet still ached and she knew it. Was this another one of her ways to punish him for not taking part earlier in the week?

"I'm afraid I'm going to have to pass," he told her.

She looked at him and said, "No one else can back out or this won't work."

"What won't work?" Austin asked warily.

"The human spiderweb. We need an even number," she explained.

His skepticism must have shown in his face for Ed Patterson said, "You're going to do it, aren't you, Mr. Bennett?"

Austin could feel five pairs of eyes on him, waiting for his answer. As much as he wanted to refuse to be a part of any of Kacy Judd's games, he knew that if he backed out, the exercise wouldn't happen. "Sure, I'll give it try," he reluctantly conceded, noticing the glimmer of surprise in Kacy's eyes.

When everyone was standing in a circle, she said, "Extend your left hand across the circle and take the left hand of the person who is opposite from you."

As it turned out, the person directly across from Austin was Kacy. He reached for her hand, which felt surprisingly soft in his. Despite all her work with the horses, her skin felt smooth, but her grip was firm. Her eyes met his and he wondered if she felt the same tingle he did.

She looked away and said, "Now with your right hand, take the hand of someone else." When they stood with their arms interlocked, she said, "Okay. Now the challenge is to unravel the spiderweb without letting go of anyone's hands. When we're finished, we should have a circle with each of us holding the hands of the persons standing next to us."

Just great, Austin thought. If it wasn't bad enough that his bones ached, now she wanted to twist them into unnatural positions. "Have you done this before?" he asked, trying not to sound as irritable as he felt.

"The answer is yes. Trust me. It works," Kacy responded cheerfully.

Everyone stood motionless, looking as uncomfortable as Austin felt. It was obvious no one wanted to be the one to initiate any movement. Finally, Kacy said, "Ed, what if you step over the arms connecting Sharon and Frank?"

Carefully, Ed did as she suggested, which created an even bigger tangle in Austin's opinion. Frank made a move that resulted in Austin being pushed back to back with Kacy. Several moves later they were face to face, which had Austin's heart pounding and his blood racing. He was close enough to feel her warm breath on his cheek.

"This isn't going to work." Austin tried to extricate himself, but Kacy refused to let go of his hand. Sharon, too, clung fast, not relinquishing her grip, either.

"No, don't stop now. We're just about there," Ed pleaded.

To Austin's amazement, the others seconded his plea to continue. He had no choice but to work at untangling their limbs until they were finally standing side by side in a circle with their hands connected.

"Hey! We did it!" several voices proclaimed in joyful surprise.

"Good job!" Kacy praised them effusively for their perseverance, which had everyone congratulating one another. Austin thought they acted as if they'd figured out the key to cold fusion.

"All right. Time to evaluate," Kacy announced, motioning for everyone to sit back down on the ground.

Evaluate? Austin wanted nothing more than to take his weary bones back to the lodge. Since that wasn't possible, the next best thing would be to find his own little corner of wilderness and climb into the sleeping bag. However, once again all eyes were upon him as he was the only one still standing. He had no choice but to sit.

"What behavior contributed to the success of getting untangled?" Kacy asked.

All the answers were similar. Frank said...Ed said...Sharon said... Of course Austin's name was not mentioned. He hadn't come up with anything that had helped them. How could he? He was in pain. All he had wanted to do was let go.

"What hindered you?" was Kacy's second question.

Austin felt like a fish swimming in a small glass bowl. No one said a word, but he knew what they were thinking and he figured the only reason why no one spoke was out of fear of offending the boss.

Finally Ed was brave enough to say, "I think you need a positive attitude. If one person doesn't think it'll work, it slows the rest of us down."

Austin knew the remark was directed at him. Feeling rather foolish, he pierced Kacy Judd with a stinging glare. He knew she had to be enjoying his discomfort, but to his surprise, she simply said, "Sometimes when you're working as a team someone has a legitimate reason to be skeptical."

Austin wanted to agree with her. He should have told them that every bone in his body ached, every muscle felt as if it had been through a wringer. He didn't. In this instance, he had no right to be the wet blanket on their success.

"I have to admit, I would have quit if the rest of you hadn't taken a positive attitude," he finally said. "Maybe the lesson to be learned here is that even when one person has a bad attitude, it doesn't necessarily mean failure. You just can't give up."

His remark earned him positive comments from the others, but it was Kacy's look of respect that stuck with him long after the discussion had ended.

With the fire diminishing to a few glowing embers, Kacy passed out sleeping bags and assigned everyone a chore for in the morning. The thought of sleeping in the presence of five other people made Austin uneasy. He would have preferred to spread his sleeping bag as far away as possible, but the others lay in a semicircle, reminding Austin that they really did consider themselves a team.

Once everyone was settled, Kacy announced, "All right listen up. It looks pretty clear tonight, but if it should rain before morning, we head for the cabin. Otherwise, I'll see you at sunrise for breakfast."

Austin stifled a groan. This wasn't supposed to be a vacation, but sunrise? He slid into the sleeping bag and looked up at the sky. Never in his life had he seen so many glittering points of light. He wasn't the only one amazed by their numbers.

"I can't believe how many stars there are," Caroline said quietly. She was at least fifteen feet away from Austin, but in the still night air her voice carried as if she were right beside him. "It's almost as if we were in the planetarium."

Even Austin had to admit that the starlit sky was quite a spectacle. To his surprise, he found it peaceful lying beneath it, and for the first time in a long time the last thing on his mind before he fell asleep was not work.

KACY COULDN'T BELIEVE how different Austin Bennett looked in repose. Gone were the harsh lines of skepticism and the arrogant brow. Even with a stubble of dark whiskers lining his jaw, he looked handsome. She felt her heart did a funny little kick.

She mentally scolded herself. What was she doing staring at the man anyway? If he were to wake and see her, she'd feel like a fool.

Maybe she was a fool for even caring what he thought of her. But every time those blue eyes glanced in her direction she wanted to prove something to him. What it was, she wasn't sure, but something.

As she always did on the morning of the camp out,

she gave the wake up call, clanging a metal bar against a triangle. Standing as far away from Austin's sleeping bag as possible, she continued to make noise until everyone was awake.

"Breakfast will be here in about fifteen minutes," she announced, then watched as bodies scurried for the bushes and the creek. Roughing it was the least favorite part of the course and Kacy knew that in every group there was at least one person who had trouble coping without the modern conveniences offered at the lodge. This trip it was Caroline. Kacy had seen her stuff a makeup pouch in her saddlebag before they had left the ranch. When Caroline made a dash for the corral, Kacy had no doubt as to the reason why.

By the time the chuck wagon had arrived with their breakfast, Caroline wore a clean cotton T-shirt. Besides changing, she had put on her makeup which Kacy knew meant she had used cold water and a compact mirror.

To Kacy it wasn't worth the hassle. Working on the ranch she seldom worried whether her clothes were clean and her makeup fresh. To her surprise, most of the guests at the ranch appreciated the freedom from having to worry about such things. And some, like Caroline, didn't.

The only other person who hadn't been able to leave civilization behind was Austin. Kacy knew that he had brought his cellular phone along and once last night when he thought no one was looking, she had seen him pull out his palmtop. The man never stopped thinking about work and again she wondered what it was that Daphne saw in him—other than a gorgeous specimen of man, that is.

For he was that—even in wrinkled clothes and with an unshaven jaw. A scowl creased his cheeks until Kacy announced that DJ, the Triple J's chef, would be cooking breakfast for everyone. Using a portable gas stove, the cook impressed the campers with his outdoor culinary skills, making fresh raspberry crepes.

As soon as breakfast was over, Kacy made her last announcement. "You have one final assignment." She didn't miss the grimace on Austin Bennett's face and enjoyed saying, "Pile all the dirty dishes into the wagon, roll up your sleeping bags and make sure you leave the place just as you found it. We'll be heading out at nine o'clock."

Sighs of relief greeted her announcement. By five minutes past nine, everyone was at the corral except Austin. Normally Kacy wouldn't have been concerned with a few minutes delay, but dark clouds gathered in the western sky. She called out his name but there was no response.

"Do you want me to go look for him?" Ed Patterson offered. "It could be he's in the woods."

The horses were restless. Kacy knew the gray sky meant rain was on its way. If they waited any longer, they would risk getting caught in a thunderstorm. They needed to get back to the ranch.

"Maybe he's down by the creek." Kacy called out his name again but there was no response. She turned to Ed. "I'll tell you what. You take the woods, I'll check the creek." To the others she said, "And if he shows up here, tell him to stay put."

Kacy marched toward the creek, anxiety worming its way into her conscience. Where was the man? Not once had she lost a camper, but then never had she had one like Austin Bennett.

Again, she called out his name. Finally, as she nearly slid down the bank of the creek, she saw him. He was sitting on a huge rock at the water's edge and he was on the phone! Anger rushed through her. She marched on over to where he sat, her hands on her hips.

"What do you think you're doing?"

He covered the mouthpiece and said, "This is an important call."

"You're keeping your team waiting," she said caustically.

He gave her a steely look. "I said this is an important call."

"I'm sure you believe that every word you utter is important, Mr. Bennett, but frankly I don't care about your importance. What I care about is getting six people back to the ranch before the storm that's building in the west dumps a whole lot of rain and maybe hail on us."

He looked up at the sky. "It's sunny."

"It won't be for long."

"I'll be there in five minutes." He turned his back to her, dismissing her as though she were one of his peons at the factory.

Trying to maintain a grip on her patience, Kacy took a deep breath, then started back up the hill. However she stopped suddenly when she heard Austin's next sentence.

"Jean, you're too good to me. I'll bring back something special for you."

Jean? He was talking to a woman? This was what was so important that he had everyone else waiting on him? Anger she had managed to keep at bay came rushing out.

She marched over to the boulder where he sat, grabbed the cellular phone from his hands and tossed it across the creek. It landed in the tall grass, disappearing from sight. Kacy knew it was an irrational act, one done solely out of her bad temper, but it made her feel oh so good to see the look on Austin's face.

"That's what I think of your *important* call, Mr. Bennett," she declared bravely. "When I said there were no cell phones at the ranch, I meant there were no cell phones. Now get your city butt up that hill and back to the corral or you can find your own way home." She spun around and started up the embankment.

She didn't get far. He was in front of her in a flash, towering over her with a look on his face that could only be described as dangerous. Besides the fact that he was a good six inches taller than she was, the fact that they were going up hill and that he was ahead of her meant she was at an even greater disadvantage.

"You think you can just throw my phone across the creek?" His voice was dangerously calm.

"I just did," she said boldly.

"Yeah, and now you're going to go get it."

"No, I'm not."

"Yes, you are." He grabbed her by the arm and pulled her toward the creek.

"Stop this! Take your hands off me or I'll…" she trailed off realizing that she had truly gotten herself into a predicament. What would she do? Kick him? Knee him? He was clearly in command and her anger changed to fear.

"Or you'll what? Scream for someone to come rescue you from the big bad city guy who's trying to get you to retrieve a piece of his personal property that you so recklessly tossed across the creek?"

He continued to push her bucking body toward the water. When it was obvious he meant what he said, she pleaded with him, "Let me take off my boots."

He ignored her plea, dragging her into the creek. She

kicked and splashed, fighting him all the way. Water seeped into her boots and up her calves. She pounded him with her fists, but it had no effect, the arm around her waist as tight as a vise.

They were almost to the other side when he stumbled, dragging her down with him. Together they fell into the water where he was finally forced to release his grasp.

She immediately got to her feet, shaking with fury. She swayed and he was there to steady her with a hand on her shoulder which she immediately slapped away. "Look what you've done! I'm all wet!" she cried out.

If she expected an apology, she was in for disappointment. "And whose fault is that? If you hadn't been kicking and twisting we wouldn't have fallen."

She couldn't say a word. She was too angry. She slogged through the water toward the opposite bank of the creek.

"Where are you going?" he called after her.

"You think I'm not going to get that damn phone after all this?" She tossed back over her shoulder. He followed her and tried to grab her by the arm but she slipped away.

"Forget about the phone," he ordered.

Kacy took orders from no man, and especially not this one. She kept sloshing through the creek until she reached the other side. Once on land, she sat down and pulled off her boots, one at a time. In an exaggerated motion, she poured the water out of them, letting him know by her glare that he was indeed responsible.

Then she tugged them back on and went in search of the cell phone. He tagged along behind her.

"Will you stop this? I told you it's not important. It's easily replaced." The tone of his voice matched the scowl on his face.

She paid no attention, but kept kicking aside the tall grass in search of the phone until finally he grabbed her by the arm and turned her around. "All right. Enough is enough. I don't want the phone. All I want right now is to get back to the lodge and into some dry clothes and shoes that don't squish when I walk."

"They wouldn't be squishing if you had dumped the water out," she chastised him, glancing down at his feet.

"That doesn't change the fact that we're both soaking wet," he said, his eyes roving up and down her figure and coming to rest on her chest. It was then that something changed in his face. Gone was exasperation, replaced by a very different emotion.

Kacy shivered and not because she was wet. One glance at her shirt told her it was like a piece of window glass, revealing everything inside it. Austin Bennett could see the outline of her satin bra. But even worse, her nipples were clearly revealed, made prominent by the cold. Startled, she met his gaze.

Suddenly the air was thick with tension, only this time it wasn't anger making it difficult to breathe. It was a sexual awareness so powerful that neither one of them spoke. They just stood there trying to figure out why their bodies were sending out signals to each other that neither one had any business sending the other. No matter how hard Kacy tried to ignore the feelings, they urged her to imagine what it would be like to feel Austin Bennett's large hands all over her wet body.

She lowered her eyes, afraid he might be able to see what thoughts were racing through her head. It was too late. His mouth swooped down on hers, capturing it with an intensity that had Kacy's heart feeling as if it would jump right out of her chest. Even though her clothes were wet, she felt on fire as he kissed her hungrily, deeply, exploring her mouth with his lips and his tongue.

Her hands flew to his face and she kissed him back, wanting to ignore everything but the wild, urgent need unfurling inside her. She soon discovered it was a need echoed in him as he pulled her tightly against him and she felt his rock-hard arousal.

Using willpower she didn't know she had, she managed to push him away. He didn't protest, but simply stood there, eyes dark with emotion, lips parted.

"What was that for?" She tried to sound offended, but she knew she had failed.

Then the familiar sarcastic chuckle returned. "As if you don't know."

"I don't," she insisted, stiffening her spine.

"Whatever," he said, then turned and started to walk away. "I'm going back."

She watched him scramble down the small embankment and back into the slowly moving water of the creek. Kacy followed him. He waited for her at the other side and they walked side by side back to the corral, but neither said a word.

"Oh my gosh! What happened?" Caroline asked when they got back.

The thunderous look on Austin's face told them it was a question that wasn't going to get answered. So Kacy was the one who replied.

"Just a little mishap. Nothing serious." She glanced again at the sky which was becoming more ominous with each passing minute. "I suggest we get moving. Now."

"But you're all wet."

"So will you be if we don't hurry."

That had everyone eager to follow her instructions.

As they headed back, Kacy could hear Caroline trying to discreetly discover the reason both he and Kacy had returned to camp soaking wet. Kacy listened closely, trying to hear just how much of the story he'd repeat to the other members of the group.

To Kacy's both surprise and relief he simply said, "It was nothing. Really."

Then she wondered if he was talking about their dunk in the creek or their kiss.

Chapter Six

As Kacy had predicted, a thunderstorm swept across the prairie and onto the Triple J shortly after they arrived back at the ranch. By the time the horses had been groomed and put away, the rain fell in a steady downpour. While they watched it from the entrance to the barn, Kacy clapped her hands to get everyone's attention.

"All right, listen up, team. I expect this thundershower will have moved out of here shortly, which means we'll be getting together this afternoon for our final team event, the rodeo."

Rodeo? The mere mention of the word caused Austin to picture bucking broncs and beastly bulls tossing human beings into the air as if they were rag dolls. It was not a pleasant image and certainly not one he wanted to be a part of. Certainly she couldn't mean that they, the newly trained horse riders, were actually to take part in such an activity? Suddenly the bleachers and the chutes he had seen at one of the corrals made sense.

"We'll be competing in teams and I have to tell you, I like to win. So I've scheduled a practice session so I can give you some tips that will help us do just that—win!" Kacy told the group.

Practice? Austin had an uneasy feeling in the pit of his stomach.

"What kind of rodeo is this?" he asked, his instinct for self-preservation overruling his ego that begged him not to ask a foolish question.

"An amateur one," Kacy answered, with a grin she shared with everyone but him. As if they all shared a private joke which he didn't understand, she looked at him apologetically and said, "Oh—that's right. You missed the beginning of the program—when everybody else was learning how to be a cowboy—or cowgirl."

"Then you're saying I shouldn't bother with this rodeo thing," he stated unequivocally.

"Of course you should. As a matter of fact, you have to. We need you." She turned to the others and added, "Don't we?"

All heads nodded, a few voices mumbled agreement. Austin knew right then and there he should tell them they would just have to do this rodeo stuff without him. He should have.

But he didn't.

He couldn't because he knew it was what Kacy Judd wanted him to do. He could see it in her eyes and the challenging tilt of her chin. She expected him to back out of the last and final event. Well, he wasn't going to give her the satisfaction.

"Then count me in," he told her, annoyed by how easy it was for her to push his buttons.

"Are you sure you want to do this, Mr. Bennett? I mean, the rest of us have been practicing all week long…" she trailed off in a way that made it sound as if she didn't think he could do it.

"I said I'll do it, Ms. Judd, and I will." There was a steeliness to his voice he had no control over.

"Great. What we need to do is decide who's doing what." She pulled a clipboard from the wall and flipped a piece of paper over and began to write. "First event is the spoon race. We need our steadiest rider for this."

"That would be Sharon," someone stated.

"I agree. Sharon it is." Kacy wrote on the clipboard, then asked, "What about the ribbon tying?"

Caroline raised her hand. "Put me down for that. I'd rather chase around a goat than try to do anything on horseback."

Ed Patterson's hand went up next. "And I'll do the calf roping. I actually managed to get one the other day when we were herding the cattle."

"I'll take the obstacle course." Austin saw Paul Mayer raise a hand and volunteer.

"Okay, that leaves being a clown or riding Old Yellow," Kacy declared when only two positions remained. "I'd better take Old Yellow so that means Austin will be a clown. How does that sound?" She looked at Austin, waiting for a response.

Austin could only stare at her in disbelief. She actually believed he'd get dressed up as a clown so his employees could laugh at him? He could feel all eyes on him as Kacy waited for him to respond.

"Is there a reason why I can't ride Old Yellow?" he asked.

"That wouldn't be a good idea," she stated in a voice that refused any protests.

That didn't matter to Austin. "Why not?"

"Because you only rode a horse for the first time yesterday and riding Old Yellow is an event we normally only assign to experienced riders. Since everyone in this group is a beginner, it's better if I do it."

"What about the other groups? Does this mean that you'll be competing against your brothers?"

"No."

"In other words, a Bennett employee is going to be riding in the last event for the other two teams, but we have to have one of the staff represent us."

"It's different for them. This week wasn't the first time they sat on a horse."

Austin could feel every macho nerve in his body reacting to the situation. She was deliberately pointing out his inadequacy, making him feel as if she had measured him and he had come up short. "You said this is an amateur rodeo. We're *all* amateurs. Is it a fair competition if we have a professional do one of our events for us?"

"Are you saying you want to ride Old Yellow?" Kacy looked at him as if he had just suggested he ride naked with no saddle.

"I believe I can do it," Austin answered.

"Yeah! Go for it, sir," Caroline rooted him on.

The sir rankled, but Austin was grateful the others backed her up, adding their "You can do its" as a vote of confidence.

"I think the *team* has spoken, Ms. Judd," Austin remarked.

She hesitated before saying, "Very well. It's your life, but don't say I didn't warn you." She tempered the warning with a smile.

Austin didn't see how he could be in any danger. For goodness' sake. This was a dude ranch offering corporate retreats…not a training camp for future rodeo stars. And if two of his employees were willing to risk riding the horse, why shouldn't he?

As the rain gradually diminished, everyone headed

back to the lodge. Austin was about to leave when Kacy stopped him.

"If you're serious about the rodeo, I suggest you come to the practice as soon as we've finished lunch. Corral C. I can't put you on Old Yellow. It wouldn't be fair, but I'll let you try riding Blue Jeans. If you can stay on him, you'll stay on Old Yellow."

"What do you mean, stay on?"

She nodded. "That *is* the object."

"Well I don't plan on falling off."

She chuckled. "No one *plans* to fall off a bucking bronc."

"A what?" he asked, his eyes narrowing.

"A bucking bronc. That's what Old Yellow is."

"You expect me to ride a bucking bronc?" he asked in disbelief.

"No, *I* didn't expect you to do a damn thing around here. *You* were the one who volunteered." She shoved her fists to her waist in that maddening way that had her already wet shirt straining at the seams. "Now, if you want to back out, just say so. I'm sure your team would understand. After all, they've made it through most of the week without you."

She spun around and walked away from him. He wanted to toss some nasty remark out at her, but he couldn't think of a single thing to say. There was only one thing on his mind as he watched her sashay back to the lodge in wet jeans that clung to her shapely figure in a most tantalizing way. The memory of that kiss at the creek and what it was like to hold her wet body close to his. He could still feel the heat.

AUSTIN HAD EVERY intention of going to the rodeo practice. The thought of getting on a bucking bronc without knowing the first thing about it was enough to humble even him.

However, during lunch he had received a message that he call Jean as soon as possible. He wouldn't have returned the call until later that afternoon, but earlier his secretary had called threatening to quit her job if his father continued to intrude in her life.

In his typical fashion, his father had taken it upon himself to run things during his absence. Unfortunately he included Jean in that category. Austin knew that his father and his secretary had never worked well together. It was one of the reasons why Austin was so fond of the older woman. She was one person his father couldn't turn against him.

So Austin made the phone call and as it turned out, was able to calm the tempest in a teacup for the second time. However, their conversation reminded him that when he returned to Chicago he would once more face the stress of being the CEO of Bennett Industries. Having been away this past week had made him realize just how much pressure that was.

Just as Austin was about to leave for the corral, the phone rang. Thinking it was Jean calling with one last word, he answered it. It was Daphne.

"Darling, please don't hang up. We need to talk."

The "darling" grated on his nerves. "Daphne, I can't talk. I'm already fifteen minutes late to a meeting."

"But what about tomorrow?"

"What about it?"

"You still want me to pick you up at the airport, don't you?"

"I don't want you to fight all that traffic. I'll take a cab."

"It's no trouble. Darling, I need to see you. We need

to be together. To talk...to make love. I'm going to do
all sorts of wonderful things to that big, strong body of
yours. I bet those muscles need some tender loving care,
don't they?''

''Daphne, I really can't talk right now.''

She wasn't about to let him end the conversation.
''Hush. Just listen to this. You can stretch out on my
satin sheets and I'll get some of that sesame oil and work
it into those muscles that have been bruised. I'll run my
hands all over that big body of yours...''

Austin discovered her words brought the most wonderful image to his mind. Warm oil, soft hands, caressing, smoothing, easing the tension and soreness from his
muscles. What a fantasy. Having a beautiful woman rubbing away all his worries, all his aches. Magical hands
they were, making him feel oh so good.

First his backside. Starting with his neck and shoulders, all the way down to the toes on his feet. Ah, easing
away the distress caused by those damn cowboy boots.
And when the back side was done, she'd roll him over
and....

Startled, he nearly dropped the receiver. He realized
that the tender hands giving him imaginary massage belonged not to Daphne, but to Kacy. Right now, even
though Daphne was speaking in his ear, he couldn't even
picture her in his mind. All he could think of was a sassy
cowgirl with more curves than any fashion model would
be caught dead with.

As hard as he tried, he couldn't erase that mental image of her standing in the creek, her clothing soaked,
her eyes mirrored with the same surprise that he had felt.
She had looked so vulnerable, so desirable he hadn't
been able to resist kissing her. The memory of how she
had looked created a longing deep inside him.

"Austin, are you there?"

"Yes, Kacy, I am." As soon as the words were uttered, Austin knew he had made a big mistake.

"Kacy? Who is she? Austin, are you seeing someone else? Is that why you've been treating me so badly?"

He raked a hand through his hair. "I'm sorry, Daphne. I made a slip of the tongue. That's all."

"Is she someone on the trip with you."

"Daphne, there is nobody."

"I don't believe you. Ooooh, Austin! How could you do this to me?"

"I really need to go. I was supposed to be at a meeting a half an hour ago. I'll call you next week when it's more convenient to talk."

"Next week? You think you can just call me whenever it suits you?"

She had a full head of steam up now and was going to give it to him with both barrels. He sensed it coming on.

"Well, I'm going to tell you something, Mr. Big Shot Bennett. If you think I'm going to sit around and wait for you to decide when it's convenient for you to see me, you're all wrong. If you want those stupid sore muscles of yours massaged—go to a masseuse."

The next thing Austin heard was a click. She had hung up on him. Not that he blamed her. It was the first time in his life that he had ever called a woman by the wrong name. He closed his eyes briefly and shook his head, wondering why he couldn't stop thinking of Kacy Judd.

Within seconds the phone rang again. Tempted not to answer it, Austin waited several rings before finally picking it up.

This time it was his father. After hearing Jean's version of the problem, now he had to listen to his father's long-winded interpretation. By the time he hung up, it was close to two o'clock. He had a sick feeling in the pit of his stomach that he wasn't going to find Kacy Judd out at the corral giving the team pointers.

He could have gone and found out. But the thought of arriving an hour late and seeing that impudent look on her face had him pulling out his laptop. However, as hard as he tried to concentrate on work, there was only one thing on his mind.

The image of lying naked next to Kacy Judd and having her run those capable hands all over his body.

ANY HOPE THAT the weather would prevent Austin from making a fool of himself died when he parted the blinds and saw the cloudless sky. Gone were any traces of the earlier morning rain. He sighed and reluctantly reached for the cowboy hat. As he adjusted it to just the right angle in front of the mirror, he hardly recognized himself.

Maybe he didn't make such a bad cowboy after all. Pretending he was wearing a holster, he drew imaginary guns and fired, making a hissing sound with his teeth. "Gotcha!" he boasted, then blew the smoke from the imaginary pistols before slipping them back into their holster.

"Yeah, Austin, you would have made one mean cowboy," he told his reflection, then with one more cock of the brim, headed for the corral.

The rest of his team was already there when he arrived. They all looked relieved to see him and he felt a sense of duty. Even if he didn't think the course was worthwhile, he needed to show these people they could count on him. He experienced a pang of remorse that he hadn't taken an interest in the activities earlier in the week. Maybe this rodeo was his chance to make up for that.

The first event of the afternoon was the egg and spoon race. Austin and his teammates cheered as Sharon balanced an egg on a spoon while she rode a horse from one end of the corral to the other. She moved very slowly. Fortunately, the other two competitors dropped their eggs along their way.

Their second contestant didn't fare as well. In the goat tying event, Caroline finished second. Ed Patterson also finished a second in the calf roping, with Paul Mayer coming in third on the obstacle course. Although the clowns provided entertainment, they weren't judged, which meant the winning team would be determined by the final event—riding Old Yellow.

Austin sized up his competition with a critical eye. Trent Carlisle looked as if he could be a stand-in for the guy who played Hercules on television. Austin knew the younger man spent lunch hours at the gym. Judging by the size of his biceps, Austin figured he probably went to a health club after dinner, too. And before work in the morning.

Rob Tolliver, on the other hand, looked like a couch potato. Middle-aged with a paunch supported by weekly poker games that featured beer and pizza, he was a couple of inches shorter than both Austin and Trent.

Although both men had experience riding, Austin hoped that when it came to a bucking bronc, that meant little. Finishing ahead of Rob wasn't going to be a problem but Trent gave Austin a worry.

As the last event was announced, Austin made his way over to the chutes. Until this point, Kacy hadn't said a word to him about missing the practice session.

If he thought he would escape her sarcastic tongue, he was mistaken.

"Didn't need any practice, eh?" she said with a smirk as he walked up to her.

"You know that's not true. Something came up." He decided not to try to explain why he had missed the training session. She would only make more caustic comments about being "unplugged" at the resort.

"What? A phone call from your Daphne?"

He tried to show no emotion, but he knew he looked guilty. "Are you going to tell me what to do, or not?"

She turned and nodded toward the chute. "See that horse in there? That's Old Yellow. If you stay on him longer than the other two fellows, you win."

Austin looked at the horse standing quietly in the chute. He was a golden tan with a black mane and from what Austin could see, didn't appear to be ill tempered.

Hanging over the top rail of the fence was a pair of chaps. Kacy pulled them down and handed them to Austin. "Here. These will help keep your jeans from getting ripped."

Open in the front and back, the chaps looked to Austin as if all they were going to do was accent his private parts. If he put these things on he would really look and feel like a dimestore cowboy.

When he hesitated, she asked, "Need me to do it for you?" in a saucy way that had Austin's hormones agitating.

"No."

"Good. A cowboy shouldn't need a lady to help him with his chaps. Those are called batwing chaps because they're open at the sides so you can put them on without taking off your boots," she explained.

Reluctantly, Austin pulled the leather chaps over his

jeans. He tied the beltlike fastener around his waist, then snapped together the sides.

"We should tape your wrists."

Austin followed her over to the score table where she grabbed a roll of first aid bandaging tape.

"All right. Put out your hands."

He did as she instructed, watching her fingers wind the thick, white tape around not only his wrists but most of his hands as well. As she worked, he tried not to think about the fantasy he had imagined only a short while ago.

But it was useless. As her fingers smoothed and tugged, he couldn't help but wonder what those hands would be like on other parts of his anatomy. He looked away, to the chute where Old Yellow stood passively, as if he didn't have a bucking bone in his body. He looked at the stands, where his teammates sat, hoping for victory. He looked to the sky, hoping a dark cloud would magically appear and dump a torrent of rain on him.

He looked everywhere but at Kacy, but it didn't help. He was aroused by her close proximity and those hands were… He took a deep breath and blew it out. Why did he have to be wearing pants that called attention to the one part of his anatomy affected by her ministrations?

"All set," she snapped and turned to toss the tape onto the score table. "Come on. We'll hop up on a chute and I'll show you what it's all about."

He was relieved that she didn't seem to notice his discomfort. He followed her to one of the empty wooden chutes where she motioned for him to climb up beside her.

When he was perched across from her she asked, "You ever seen a rodeo before?"

"Hasn't everybody?"

"Then you know what the object is here."

"Yeah, don't get killed."

She gave him an admonishing look. "Old Yellow will be standing there minding his own business. What you have to do is get on, making sure both hands are gripping the reins. If this were a real rodeo, you'd only use one hand and let the other fly. But since this is only for fun, you can use two."

"Fun, huh?"

"Lots of people think riding a bucking bronc is exhilarating."

He shot her a dubious look. "What do I do when I want to get off?"

She chuckled. "I don't think you'll have any trouble getting off. One thing you should remember. When you fall, try to roll. Landing flat out will knock the wind out of you."

Austin felt apprehension dance up and down every nerve in his body. "Are you sure this is safe?"

"Safe? Who said anything about it being safe?"

He looked to see if she were joking, but to his dismay there was not a glimmer of humor in her eyes.

"Scared?" she taunted him.

"Sensible would be a better word."

"It's a challenge, Mr. Bennett. Either you accept your limitations and let fear keep you stagnant where you're at or you stretch to reach new heights and discover the power conquering fear can bring. What's it gonna be?"

He knew it was now or never. This was his opportunity to back out and let his common sense keep him from making a big mistake. Instead he let his ego make the decision. "I'll stretch. I only hope I'm not going to be sorry."

"Look, we do this all the time. Old Yellow isn't your typical bucking bronc. He's not true rodeo stock, just an old horse who occasionally gets a little feisty." She glanced at her watch. "Okay, listen up. We've only got five minutes for me to tell you everything you need to know about bronc riding."

Austin figured it was probably the shortest lesson in bronc riding history. To his amazement, she gave him a step-by-step accounting of just what was going to happen and why. So reassuring was she that by the time the bronc event was to start, he actually felt confident he was going to ride Old Yellow and win the competition for his team.

All the bronc riders reached into a hat to determine who would ride first. Austin drew the yellow marker with the number one on it. Kacy handed him a pair of leather gloves and said, "Let's do it." He climbed the boards of the chute, following her instructions step by step.

As the chute gate opened, Old Yellow didn't move. A slap on the rear had him whinnying, then walking out into the corral as if there wasn't anyone on his back and he didn't have a care in the world. Austin relaxed and smiled. So this had been another one of Kacy Judd's ploys to make him anxious. So she liked to joke, did she?

He turned around and smiled at her. "Real funny." Then he let go of the reins and held up his hands in midair. "Look. No hands." Just then someone blew a bugle horn. It was Old Yellow's cue. The horse reared and sent Austin flying through the air and onto the hard ground.

Winded, he lay flat on his back, gasping for air.

"I told you to roll when you fell," were the first

words he heard. He looked up to see Kacy leaning over him. "Are you okay?"

He couldn't answer. How could he when he couldn't even breathe. He felt himself being propped up, then lifted between Kacy's and her brother's arms and dragged from the arena.

"You shouldn't have let go of the reins," Kacy continued to chastise him even though he felt miserable enough without her sharp tongue berating him.

He wanted to tell her the only reason he had released the reins had been because he thought it was a joke. Unfortunately, he was still fighting for his breath. Speaking was not an option.

"You told me you didn't want to be a clown, then you got out there on Old Yellow and goofed off," Kacy scolded him. "Did you listen to a single word I said about bronc riding?"

If it didn't hurt so bad to breathe, he would have told her exactly what he thought of her crash course. Rationally, he knew it wasn't her fault that he had fallen. He was the one who had let go and actually turned around to wave to the crowd. Gawd, he felt like such a fool. It didn't help that she was chewing him out.

When he was able to walk under his own power, he shrugged off Kacy and her brother's help. He unbuckled the chaps and tossed them at her.

"You'd need a suit of armor with air bags to ride that animal," he said irritably.

Kacy turned to her brother. "I'm going to take him to first aid."

Austin again shrugged off her attempts to lead him by the arm.

"No, you're not. I'm okay," he said sullenly.

"Then take off your hat and wave to your team. They think you're a wounded animal over here."

He did as she suggested and heard clapping and whistling. He grimaced as he tried to undo the bandages on his wrist.

"Are you sure you're okay?"

"Yes. The only thing damaged was my pride. I thought you said that was the beginner's horse."

"It is. Watch Trent." She pointed to where the Hercules lookalike sat in the chute on Old Yellow.

As the gate opened, the bronc came out bucking. Not big-time bucking, but enough to cause Trent to have a few bruises and bumps. He did manage to stay on until the buzzer sounded, however.

The third rider managed to stay on the horse only a few seconds longer than Austin. Instead of landing on his back, however, he slid off the horse and landed on his feet. Now Austin really felt like a loser. Even pot-bellied Rob had done better than he.

Austin's mood was a sour one as he made his way back to the bleachers. Despite the sympathetic inquiries, he knew that his team members were more disappointed that they lost than worried about his physical condition. They should have considered themselves lucky. Had he seen Trent and Rob go flying through the air he wouldn't have ridden at all. Team or no team.

As much as he wanted to disappear into his room and skip the barbecue, he knew he had to attend the event. Although the chicken and ribs received rave reviews, they couldn't make up for the humiliation Austin had suffered.

Later that evening, as he lay in bed, he couldn't stop thinking about his performance. Rational or not, he blamed Kacy.

Ever since he had arrived she had been taunting and challenging him, making him go crazy at times and causing him to act out of character. What was worse was that rather than wanting to get as far away from her as possible, he desired her. He didn't understand it...how he could be so totally annoyed by a woman one minute, then want her in his bed the next?

It was a good thing he was leaving tomorrow morning. Yet the thought of going home brought little comfort. What waited for him at Bennett Industries put a knot of anxiety in his chest. For seven years he had been working night and day, chewing antacid tablets as if they were candy and what did he have to show for it? A fancy brownstone on Astor Avenue? A closet full of designer suits? A sports car in his garage?

Again his thoughts turned to Kacy. How she took pleasure in watching one of her horses graze. In sitting on a hay bale telling a story. In watching the sunrise over the prairie. As much as he hated to admit it, he longed to find that kind of contentment in such simple things.

Could it be that he had worked so long and so hard without a vacation he had forgotten how to enjoy the simple pleasures of life? Maybe Jean was right to suggest he take a couple of weeks off and go visit his cousins in Montana. Maybe he could recapture some of the joys of life. Clear his head of the jadedness that seemed to be his constant companion.

It was a tempting thought, but the reality was his father expected him home tomorrow. *Duty.* It had always been a motivating factor in Austin's behavior. He knew that many people thought he hated his father—a natural assumption considering the way the two of them argued over the company.

What most people didn't know was that when Austin's mother died twenty years ago, he and his father had had to establish a new relationship. One that didn't include his mother as the buffer between them. For that's what she had been. Always playing the mediator, trying to keep the peace between two people whom she said were two of a kind.

Austin's father's way of coping with her death was to send his son away to a prep school. To teach him how to be a man, to prepare him for the future as the head of Bennett Industries. Of course that didn't come without a price. The preparation had to be accomplished according to his father's instructions.

Austin had learned how to be a successful man. He had also learned that no matter how much he and his father disagreed, there was a deep love and respect between them. He just wished he could make his father understand that his vision didn't necessarily have to be Austin's vision.

But they were all each other had. Which is why he would pick up a bottle of antacid tablets and go home tomorrow. To do his duty as his father's son.

Perspiration trickled down his brow. Just the thought of going back could cause him to sweat. He got up to adjust the knob on the air conditioner. As he placed his hand in front of the vent, he realized it wasn't just work making him sweat. The air coming out was warm. He adjusted the knob until it was at the lowest setting. Still, the air continued to be warm.

"Damn." He slapped the unit with his palm, then went to call the front desk.

A half an hour later there was still no cold air. Nor was there after an hour. Or two. The maintenance man gave up trying to repair the unit sometime around one in the morning.

Austin kicked off his covers. Still he sweated. And tossed and turned. No amount of complaining could get him a different room. The Triple J did provide him with a small oscillating fan. It was the best they could do—plus apologize for the inconvenience.

Inconvenience? Austin mulled over their definition of inconvenience. Punishment would have been a more apt description for his stay in the room. It was a fitting end to a week that had been full of inconveniences. He could just see the beautiful redhead Kacy laughing with her brothers over the fact that of all the rooms at the inn, his was the one to have the air-conditioning go kaput.

The longer he lay awake, hot, angry and tired, the more bullish he became. Never had he spent company money so foolishly. He had paid a large fee to sleep on the ground, pee in the woods and have his cell phone whipped out of his hands and thrown into knee-high grass crawling with critters he didn't even want to acknowledge existed.

Suddenly, he remembered something Jean had said. The course came with a money-back guarantee. Satisfaction or else. He knew that Jean had sent a check for half of the amount as a deposit on the course, and in his briefcase was a check for the second half which he was supposed to pay tomorrow at checkout.

Supposed to, were the operative words. *He* was not a satisfied customer. He was not convinced the course was worthwhile. Then why should *he* pay?

"Because you're an honest man, Austin Bennett and no matter how sour you are, you know the Triple J fulfilled its end of the agreement," a little voice in his head reminded him.

Well, he wasn't going to pay. At least not tomorrow. He would hold them to their word. Money-back guarantee. He'd mail the balance due after he was back in Chicago. Give Ms. Kacy Judd a few days to sweat over the money.

So she thought she had gotten the better of him, did she? Well, just wait until tomorrow morning. Sexy swagger or not, she was in for a lesson in dealing with city slickers. And he was just the man to give it to her.

Chapter Seven

Kacy was never so happy to see the company vans haul away the guests as she was that Friday morning. It had been a long and difficult week, thanks to one particularly difficult guest—Austin Bennett. She could still recall that icy glare he had fixed her with before getting into the van.

He hadn't said one word to her since the rodeo. Not only had he avoided her at the barbecue last night, but at breakfast this morning as well. Every other member of the team had stopped to say a few words of parting. Not the high and mighty Mr. ''Too Big for his Britches'' Bennett.

Maybe that's what bothered her even more than his stubborn refusal to be a member of the team. Kacy wasn't used to being ignored by anyone. And especially not by men. Austin had thrown her in the creek, ogled her wet body, kissed her until she thought her wet clothes would steam and now he was acting as though she didn't even exist.

She wished now that she had slapped him silly instead of asking, ''What was that for?'' Because his answer, ''As if you don't know'' only proved that he was conceited enough to think that any woman who looked him in the eye was asking to be kissed.

Unfortunately, in her case he was right. She *had* wanted him to kiss her. That was what was so irritating about the entire incident. As much as she hated to admit it, she had given him a signal inviting his lips to cover hers.

It had been a knockout of a kiss, making her all tingly and creating an ache in her that had her imagining all sorts of other magical things he could do to her body. She shivered at the memory and pushed it from her mind. There was no point in fantasizing over someone she would never see again.

As she walked back into the office she was grateful for the blast of cool air that greeted her. Suzy sat at the front desk, stuffing envelopes.

She took one look at Kacy and said, "It's going to be a hot one today, isn't it?"

"You're lucky you get to work in air-conditioning," she told her sister.

"At least it's working. I heard Mr. Bennett's unit went down last night. No wonder he was so grouchy this morning."

"He was grouchy every morning he was here," Kacy pointed out irritably.

"He was a little moody, but I wouldn't exactly call him grouchy."

Kacy gave her sister a censorious look. "He was grouchy. He didn't want to be here and he did every thing he could to make sure everyone knew it." She picked up the reservations book and sighed. "I hope these insurance people coming next week aren't as difficult."

"We'll find out on Sunday." She finished the pile of

envelopes she had been stuffing and put a rubber band around the bunch. "You going near the post office?"

"Sure. I'll stop on my way to the bank. Where's the deposit for this week?"

"Uh-oh. You haven't heard, have you?"

"Heard what?"

"There is no check to deposit this morning. Austin Bennett refused to pay the balance of his bill. Said he wasn't satisfied with the service he received."

Kacy slammed the leather-bound appointment book down on the desk. "You're joking, right?" she asked, although one look at Suzy's face told her that it was indeed true.

"Uh-uh. I was here. You should have heard the stink he made. Not even Dad could soothe his ruffled feathers."

Anger spiked Kacy's blood pressure. "He wasn't satisfied? After all the crap he pulled he's got the gall to complain about the service? Why that no-good, two-timing city slicker."

"Your neck is turning red," her sister warned her.

"And so it should. I'm so mad I could…" She made a sound of frustration and began pacing back and forth in the small office. "I should have known he would make trouble. I suppose he mentioned my name in his complaint."

Although Suzy didn't confirm it, she didn't deny it either. "He just wasn't happy, Kacy. It's not about anything one person did."

Angry as she now was, Kacy wasn't about to admit that she might have contributed to Austin Bennett's dissatisfaction. Besides, she really hadn't done anything to warrant the Triple J not getting paid. *He* was the one who had behaved unprofessionally. He had done everything in his power to sabotage the program and then had the gall to say it hadn't worked!

She took a deep breath to control her fury. "After everything we did to accommodate him..." She shook her head. "Gawd, how I hate men like that."

"It is kinda hard to believe. I mean we've never had anyone refuse to pay. And I actually thought he kinda liked you."

"What?" she shrieked.

"Now don't have a kitten on me. All I'm saying is that I have this sort of sixth sense when it comes to reading people." Suzy twirled a long strand of blond hair as she explained. "Well, whenever the two of you were in the same room there seemed to be this 'energy' that moved between you."

"That wasn't energy. That was hatred," Kacy spat out.

"I don't know. If you ask me, he looked at you the way a guy looks at a woman he wants to dance with between the sheets."

Kacy hated the tingle of pleasure her sister's words produced. "Austin Bennett is the last man I'd want interested in me. He's a jerk and I can't believe Dad didn't make him pay up."

"Don't blame Dad. He did everything he could to try to get the money out of him, but I don't think anyone could have gotten that guy to change his mind. He was determined not to pay."

Kacy stopped pacing and faced her sister. "He's not going to get away with this."

"What are you going to do?" Suzy asked wide-eyed.

"I don't know, but I'll think of something. There's got to be some legal recourse. I mean, we fulfilled *our* end of the bargain. He's the one who wouldn't fulfill his.'' She walked over to the file cabinet. ''What about that agreement he signed?''

''I don't know about any of that legal stuff. All I know is that Dad and Dusty were talking about how they shouldn't have put that money-back guarantee stuff into the brochure,'' Suzy answered.

Kacy grimaced. ''I told Dusty not to put that in.'' She groaned. ''If he had dealt with some of the people I had to do business with in New York, he wouldn't have put it in. But he's so sure that everyone's going to appreciate the beauty of the ranch.'' She shook her head disconsolately.

''At least we have half the money,'' Suzy offered as consolation.

''Half? We deserve double for what that man has put me through this week!'' She grabbed a set of keys from the desk and headed for the door.

''Where are you going?''

''To the airport. I might not be able to get the money out of that city slicker, but I'm damn well going to make sure he gets a piece of my mind before he leaves.''

''I don't think you'll make it. The vans left over an hour ago.''

Kacy didn't care if she had to do a hundred miles an hour all the way to Grand Forks. She'd make it before their plane left.

And she would have…had it not been for the flat tire she had before she'd gone even a quarter of the way there. She glanced at the clock and groaned. She'd never make it to the airport now.

''Damn!'' She slammed her palms against the steering wheel. She sat for a moment, eyes shut, head bowed. There had to be a way for her to get even. But what? As she climbed out to assess the damage done to her tire, she told herself that one way or another, she'd pay back Austin Bennett—or her name wasn't Kacy Judd.

MOST OF THE Bennett employees wore western wear on their way home. Not Austin. He needed to look like the CEO of Bennett Industries, not some weekend cowboy. Although he had packed his jeans and boots in his suitcase, the cowboy hat had been left behind at the lodge—along with the memories of one particular cowgirl who had made his life miserable.

As he glanced about the waiting area, he noticed both Sharon and Caroline wore long denim skirts and vests similar to the ones Kacy Judd had worn the first night they had met. But the outfit just didn't look the way it had on Kacy.

At the memory Austin felt a stirring in his loins. Why was it that no matter how hard he tried, he couldn't stop thinking about the woman? Everything he looked at seemed to remind him of her. Even now, waiting in the airport he couldn't stop thinking about that night she had picked him up wearing that big yellow slicker.

Nothing had seemed quite the same since then. Certainly not his mood. Nor his attitude toward work. Or his feelings for Daphne. He didn't understand how so many things could change in only five days.

He got up to call his father's number, only to get the housekeeper who reported that Henry Bennett was out playing golf. Austin knew that if his father was playing golf it wasn't for pleasure's sake, but for business. He popped a couple of antacids into his mouth and tried not to think about what waited for him in Chicago.

He wondered what it would be like not to have any responsibilities, to be able to get up each day and not even think about what was happening at the office. Not once in his thirty-one years had he taken a vacation on the spur of the moment. He had been too busy trying to get ahead, to prove himself to his father, to the world. He hadn't been able to afford the luxury of being impulsive.

Now he was standing in the middle of the airport, contemplating what it would be like to not return to Chicago. He found it rather ironic that five days ago he hadn't wanted to come to North Dakota. Now he didn't want to leave.

He got up and walked over to the glass windows to stare out at the skyline. Nothing but flat land and bright sunshine. If he were to get in a car and drive, he bet he could drive a long ways without running into any people.

When his flight was called, Austin's sense of duty steered him toward the boarding gate. Once outside, the hot summer wind sent a few straw hats sailing. Austin's tie came loose and flapped against his cheek. He tucked it back in place, waiting while those in front of him climbed the steps to the plane.

"I think it was the best seminar I've ever attended," he overhead someone say. "For once the company spent money on something we can use."

Guilt stung Austin just as the tiny grains of sand carried by the wind stung his cheeks. Judging by the conversation around him, he knew there was no doubt about it. The consensus of the group was that the team-building experience at the Triple J had been a positive one. "Worth every penny," as one employee said in passing.

Guilt invaded Austin's conscience like a snake slithering through the grass. Ever since he had left the Triple J with the check tucked inside his suit coat he had been wrestling with his conscience. Even though he planned to send the balance of the fee in the mail, he had led the Judds to believe he wasn't going to pay. Last night, hot and tired, his ego bruised, it had seemed like a good idea to withhold the payment. Inconvenience them a little. But now, after time to think about it, his actions seemed petty. And he was not a petty man.

"You can go ahead, sir."

Austin didn't realize he was holding up the line until Rob Toliver gave his elbow a gentle nudge. He climbed the steps to the plane. Despite the flight attendant's efforts to make him comfortable, he was about as uneasy as he had been when he had got up on Old Yellow. He set his briefcase in the overhead compartment and tried to relax, but it was useless.

When he looked through the small window he saw freedom. And a chance to redeem himself. Without saying a word to anyone he got up out of his seat and approached the stewardess.

"I want to get off the plane."

As AUSTIN HEADED back into the airport he had two goals. Return to the Triple J and give them the check, and then start his vacation.

There was only one problem. The check was in his pocket, but that was all he had. In his haste to get off the plane he had left his briefcase in the overhead compartment. Inside was his wallet.

That's why his first stop was a pay phone where he called his secretary. "Jean, I've decided to take a vacation."

"Could you repeat that, Austin? There must be static on the line because I thought you said you're taking a vacation."

Austin suppressed a grin. "You heard right. I've decided to take your advice and take some time off. I'm renting a car and heading out this afternoon.''

There was a long silence prompting Austin to inquire, ''Jean, are you still there?''

''Yes. It's just that you've taken my breath away. Are you feeling all right, Austin?''

Out of the corner of his eye Austin saw the plane carrying his luggage taxi away from the terminal. He knew he should feel remorse, but he only felt as if a great weight had been removed from his chest.

''My head's fine. It's my body that's a mess. I've just been through a week from hell that ended with me being thrown from a bucking bronc.''

There was a short gasp. ''Oh my! Were you hurt?''

''It's nothing that a few days of therapeutic massage can't cure.'' Immediately the picture of Kacy Judd as masseuse leaped into his mind.

''Thank God for that,'' she breathed in relief. ''Is this why you've decided to take a vacation? To get well?''

He detected the concern in her voice. ''Actually I'm taking your advice and giving my brain a rest. Maybe I'll go out west.''

''Will you look up your cousins?''

''I haven't decided. I thought I'd just play it by ear.''

''Are you sure you're all right, Austin?''

''I'm fine.'' It wasn't exactly the truth, but then he really couldn't tell what was on his mind. Jean had in many ways been like a mother to him. He didn't want her to know that he had refused to pay his bill at the Triple J.

''What about your father?'' Jean asked.

Austin sighed. ''Just tell him I'm taking a vacation and that I'll be home in a couple of weeks.''

''He'll want a report on the ranch.''

Austin sighed. He figured he'd worry about that when he was back in Chicago. "My father ought to be glad I'm taking some time off. It'll give him the opportunity to be in complete control." Suddenly he realized what this meant for Jean. "I'm sorry, Jean. I know my father gives you a hard time. If you want to take the time off, do it."

"I've already used my vacation allowance for this year."

"Take the time without pay and I'll make up the difference in your salary out of my own pocket."

"Why, Austin..." she sounded choked up, as if she might cry. "I don't know what to say..."

"Say you'll take the time off. Two weeks. If I get back before then, I'll get a temporary to help me."

"You hate temporaries."

"Just take the time off, Jean."

"Thank you, I will."

"Before you hang up I need you to do something for me. I'm afraid my luggage went on the plane without me. Inside was my wallet. I need you to wire me some money to the nearest Western Union service." He glanced across the aisle to the rental car counter. "And call ABC Rental Cars for me. Tell them I'll pick up the car here at the Grand Forks airport."

"Is there anything else you need?"

"If there is, I'll let you know. There's one other thing I want to tell you. If you don't hear from me, don't worry. I have no agenda."

Austin could hear the concern in Jean's voice. "You take care of yourself, Austin. A fall can do nasty things to a person. And be careful on the highway."

After a sufficient amount of mothering she said goodbye. As soon as he had hung up the phone, he went back to the ticket counter.

"Where's the closest Western Union service?"

A SHORT WHILE later Austin had a shiny new rental car, a pocketful of money and freedom to do whatever he pleased. His first stop was to get a vacation wardrobe.

Since he had decided to drive west, he chose clothes he thought appropriate for the trip. Instead of khakis and polos, he bought denims and sport shirts. When the clerk suggested a pair of Tony Lama boots, he took her advice. The only thing he didn't buy was a hat.

After he grabbed a sandwich from a fast-food restaurant, he tried to call one of his cousins. There was no answer. Not that it mattered. He wasn't really going to Montana to see family. He was going to get away.

But first he needed to go to the Triple J. If he were lucky, Kacy wouldn't be in the office when he arrived. Admitting he was wrong to Dusty or Mark Judd wouldn't be a problem for him. But Kacy? He figured it was better if he didn't see her again. There had been too many sparks flying between them.

He didn't understand why she had been able to get under his skin the way she had. She was nothing like the women he usually dated. She did chores Daphne would have turned her nose up at and walked away. She didn't use any two-hundred-dollar-an-ounce imported cologne. She often smelled of hay and horses, but on her it was as powerful an aphrodisiac as any perfume.

Desire stirred inside him. He had no doubt at all that she had enjoyed kissing him, yet she had pretended that she didn't know exactly why that kiss had lasted as long as it did.

Maybe that's why he couldn't stop thinking about her.

Because they had kissed and it had been the kind of kiss that could make a man forget he had ever known another woman.

The thought of the cowgirl had certain parts of his body reacting in a way he didn't need. He decided to splash some cold water on his face and then change out of his business clothes. He wanted no reminder of his job in Chicago.

He used a wayside rest stop to change, pulling on the Wrangler jeans and Tony Lama boots. He traded his white dress shirt for a pale yellow long-sleeved western shirt that snapped up the front instead of buttoned. By the time he was done, the only thing missing was the straw cowboy hat he had left in his room at the Triple J.

He tossed his old clothes into the backseat of the car and set off on his journey. He couldn't believe how good it felt to drive down the highway without having a place to be at a specific time. Freedom. It was exhilarating.

Only he wasn't free. At least not yet. Once he'd been to the Judd ranch he'd truly know the meaning of no place to go and all day to do it. So instead of heading west, he went north, toward the place only hours ago he had vowed to never return.

This was his chance to say something about who he was—not Austin Bennett the workaholic, but Austin Bennett the honorable man with a conscience. He had a chance to right a wrong, to do something that had always been difficult for him—admit he had behaved foolishly. He had never been known for his ability to express his feelings, but maybe this vacation was a good time to start changing that. People did matter to him, no matter how difficult it was for him to show it.

He passed few cars along the narrow country road.

That's why he was surprised when he saw two men dressed in bib overalls standing next to an old rusty blue pickup with its hood up. They looked hot and disgusted.

Austin knew this was his chance to practice his new code of ethics. He pulled over and got out of the car. "Can I give you a lift?"

"I'd appreciate it. Just let me get my wallet," the larger of the two told Austin, then opened the front door of the truck and leaned inside.

Austin glanced around the landscape, noting how the heat created an optical illusion on the pavement making it look as though there were a pool of water on the horizon. The slamming of the truck door had him looking back toward the pickup.

"Hop inside," he told the two men, motioning for them to get in the car. It was the last thing he said before he felt something hard hit the back of his head. Then he sank into darkness.

KACY HAD BEEN thinking about Austin Bennett far too often that afternoon. She told herself it was because she was trying to figure out how they were going to get the rest of the money he owed them, but the truth was, she couldn't stop thinking about the way her body had reacted to his down at the creek.

It was like adding insult to injury…the fact that she had enjoyed being in his arms. Especially now, since he had turned out to be such a rat.

She spent the afternoon working in the office, hoping to occupy her mind until her brother returned and she could fuss some more with him over what they were going to do about Austin Bennett's nonpayment. It was while she was in the office that one of the local deputies called.

"Kacy, it's Bill Cox. I've got someone here I think you might know. At least I hope you do."

Kacy grinned. "Don't tell me one of my horses is wandering around your pasture again."

"Oh, it's not one of your horses. It's a man. I found him on the side of the road on my way home."

"And you think I know him?"

"I'm hoping you do. You see someone knocked him out with a nasty blow to the back of his head. Verna's bandaged it up for him so he's not bleeding, but he's got another problem. Apparently the bang on the head has given him amnesia. He can't remember who he is or where he was going. I'm hoping you might be able to shed some light on his identity."

Kacy felt uneasiness curl inside her. "What makes you think I can?"

"He had one of your business cards in your pocket."

Kacy frowned. "Is he a businessman?"

"It's kind of hard to tell. That card was the only thing he had on him. No wallet, no money, no keys. Nothing. I suspect he's been robbed."

"Robbed? Bill, people don't get robbed around here."

He chuckled. "Well, maybe not as often as they do in other places, but I'm afraid there is some crime around here. That's why I have a job."

"So what are you going to do with this guy?"

"I was hoping he was one of your guests and I wouldn't have to try to trace his identity."

"That's unlikely, Bill. The last bunch just left this morning. As far as I know, they all took off in a plane." Curious, she asked, "What does he look like?"

"I'd guess he's about six-two. Dark hair, blue eyes. Good-looking fellow. I imagine if I were to call up any of the gals in town I wouldn't have any trouble finding someone who'd be willing to take him in until he gets his memory back.''

"You're not thinking *we* should take him in, are you?''

"Naw, I just hoped you'd recognize him and we'd know how to contact his kin. I doubt he's from around these parts. He's dressed like the rest of us but Verna thinks he talks like a city slicker.''

City slicker. A crazy thought went through Kacy's head. It couldn't be…no. It was preposterous to think that the man could possibly be Austin Bennett. After all, he had hated his experience at the ranch and she couldn't imagine he'd ever return to these parts even if his life depended on it.''

Still, she asked, "What's he wearing?''

"Wrangler jeans, a pair of boots, and a yellow shirt. But I doubt he's a ranch hand. The jeans are so stiff I doubt they've seen a washing machine yet. And his shirt's new, too.''

"Are you sure he has nothing else on him that would give you a clue as to his identity?''

"Nope. His pockets were clean except for the business card. Oh, and a bag of horehound candy.''

Kacy had a strange sensation. Horehound drops? Austin Bennett had carried a small sack of them with him wherever he went. Still, how could it possibly be the CEO of Bennett Industries?

"Bill, why don't I come over and take a look for myself. If he's someone who's been here recently, I'll recognize him. If not, you'll have to do whatever the sheriff does in such cases.''

"That sounds like a fair deal.''

"I'll be over as soon as I can get someone to cover for me in the office.'' As soon as she had hung up the phone, she looked up the number of the contact person at Bennett Industries. It was a Jean Swenson. She quickly dialed the number next to the name.

"This is Jean. How may I help you?"

"This is Kacy Judd from the Triple J Ranch in North Dakota. I was wondering if you could have Mr. Bennett call me when he gets into the office Monday morning."

"I'd be happy to leave a message for him, Ms. Judd, but I'm afraid he won't be back for two weeks. You see, he had such a wonderful time at the ranch he decided to take a holiday in your part of the country."

The woman sounded absolutely delighted...which came as no surprise to Kacy. Another two weeks without her tyrant of a boss would make anyone happy.

"Are you saying he didn't get on the plane going back to Chicago?"

"That's right. Would you like to speak to someone else?"

"Oh—that won't be necessary, thank you. I'll call back in a couple of weeks."

Kacy hung up the phone and sat mystified. Could this person with amnesia really be Austin Bennett? If it was, it would serve him right. After the way he had behaved at the ranch, he deserved a bump on the head.

Amnesia. Kacy had heard stories of people who suffered from it but never had she actually known anyone with the condition. Before leaving the office, she made one more call—this one to her grandfather, a semiretired family physician who lived not far from the ranch.

He told her that it was possible to suffer from temporary amnesia after receiving a blow to the head. He also said that there was no way of predicting when the patient's memory would return or how it would return.

Amnesia was one of those puzzling conditions that often left doctors guessing.

All the way to the Cox ranch Kacy couldn't stop thinking about the possibility that this man with amnesia could be Austin Bennett. If it was… Her mind raced with the possibility. She had said she wished she could find a way to get even with the man. Maybe this was it. After all, if he didn't remember a thing…

As soon as Kacy pulled into the drive she saw a man leaning up against the corral fence, watching a mare and her foal. Something curled in her stomach. Even from a distance she had a pretty good idea that it was Austin Bennett. He didn't lean against the fence like a regular cowboy, but stood as stiff as one of the fence posts.

As Kacy's pickup rattled across the gravel, he turned and looked in her direction briefly causing her heart to leap into her throat. It *was* Austin Bennett, looking every bit as handsome as he had the day he had kissed her. She moistened her lips, as if reliving that passionate kiss near the creek.

Then, as if there was no reason to give her any more of his attention, Austin turned back to the horses. Kacy felt as if a bucket of cold water had been tossed on her memories. She parked the truck and was greeted by Bill Cox who came down the porch steps.

"Thanks for coming over, Kacy. Our mystery man's over there." He swung an arm in the direction of the corral.

As they walked toward the split rail fence Bill said, "He seems to be a pretty decent guy. Verna's already taken a liking to him. She says if you can't identify him, she's going to make it her mission to find out who he is."

The closer they got, the faster Kacy's heart beat. Even from behind, Austin Bennett was attractive. Kacy couldn't help but notice the way his butt filled out the jeans. And the broad width of his shoulders. And the bandage on the back of his head. She felt a twinge of sympathy and quickly squashed it. This was the man who had cheated her family out of a lot of money. There was no time for sympathy—whether he was hurt, or not.

"We've been calling him Rob. Since he can't remember his name, it seemed like a good enough one to use, you know, being he was robbed and all." Bill called out the name and Austin turned around.

Kacy knew it was time to make her declaration. "His name's not Rob, Bill."

"You recognize him?"

"I sure do." She took a deep breath and said. "It's Austin Beaumont."

There. She had done it. She had set the lie in motion. She should have felt guilty, but she didn't. This was the man who had cheated her family out of a significant amount of money.

"He's one of your guests?" Bill asked.

"No. He was at the ranch the other day to see about a job. Wanted to work for us but he said he had to tie up a few loose ends and then he'd be back."

"He works for you?"

"Well, not yet, but if he had our card in his pocket I guess that means he must have been on his way back to say he wanted the position."

"You hear that, Rob?" Bill looked at Austin with a grin on his face. "This here lady knows who you are."

Kacy nearly melted at the look of gratitude Austin gave her. And when those stunning blue eyes held hers, her heart definitely flipped. Injured and with no memory,

Austin Bennett held an appeal that was far greater than the magnetism he had exerted over her as a stuffy CEO.

His eyes practically devoured her face. "You know me?"

"Not exactly, but we have met. You came to our ranch to apply for a job." She had to look away from that startlingly attractive gaze for a moment. "You don't remember?"

He shook his head. "I remember nothing. It's as if someone has erased my entire life from my memory. So who am I?"

Kacy took another deep breath before saying, "Austin Beaumont."

"Beaumont," he repeated it several times as if hoping to jog his memory. "I must be of French descent."

She shrugged. "I really can't say. You applied for a job with us a couple of days ago." She was amazed at how easy the lie came to her lips.

"I'm a cowboy." It was said with a mixture of confusion and delight.

"Ranch hand is the position you wanted."

Bill rubbed his jaw thoughtfully. "Well, ain't that something? Here we were thinking you might be some city slicker on vacation."

"No, cowboy makes sense," Austin told him. "While I've been standing here looking at this mare and her foal, I felt this...this...connection." He turned again to look at the horses. "There's something about this..." he trailed off, then shook his head. "I can't explain."

"Well, sure. You're used to working with animals. That's what that means," Bill said encouragingly.

"Did I fill out a job application?" Austin asked Kacy.

One lie leads to another. And another. A little voice in her head warned her.

"You probably did, but that's not my territory. My brother handles all the hiring," she explained, realizing that she was going to have to do some fast talking with Dusty if she were going to pull off this caper.

"Then you ought to go over to the Triple J," Bill stated eagerly. "At least you'll be able to find out some more information."

"That's exactly what I was thinking," Kacy told him, her mind racing about how she was going to get everyone at the Triple J to go along with her scheme. Her father she wasn't worried about since he would be out of town for the next two weeks. But she wondered if she had made a mistake jumping in with both feet without asking the rest of the Judds first.

Maybe, but then she also knew that if she had told them what she intended to do, there was a pretty good chance that they would have nixed her plan. This way, she was giving Austin to them as a hired hand as a fait accompli. He owed them money; she was going to collect it.

She linked her arm through Austin's and felt a tingle spread through her body. He felt it, too. She could see it in his eyes.

"You come with me, Austin. We'll see that you're taken care of," she told him as she led him to the pickup.

The first stop on her way home was her grandfather's. She may have been a bit vindictive, but she wasn't heartless. Before she put Austin to work at the ranch, she wanted to make sure he wasn't in need of any medical attention.

Then she'd give him a place to stay—not at the lodge, but in the old bunkhouse. The less time he spent around the ranch help, the less likely it would be that anyone would slip up. Besides, it wouldn't hurt him to have to rough it a bit. The bunkhouse was clean, even if it was a bit Spartan.

Clothing wouldn't be a problem. The ranch's shop had everything he needed. And she'd even let him use one of her horses. And advance him a few bucks on his salary. Hopefully his memory wouldn't return for at least two weeks. In that amount of time she could work him pretty darn hard.

"Thank you, Kacy. This is really very kind of you," Austin jerked her out of her musings.

Kind? She swallowed with a bit of difficulty. "There's no need to thank me. I'm just doing what anyone in my position would do."

WHILE HER GRANDFATHER examined Austin, Kacy went into his kitchen to call her brother Dusty and break the news to him. His reaction was pretty much what she expected.

"Kacy, have you totally flipped out?"

"The guy stiffed us for a lot of money. What's wrong with getting it back?"

"What you're planning to do is dishonest!"

"Me dishonest? What about him?"

"He wasn't satisfied with the service he got here. It's his right. Read our pamphlet."

"So he withholds *half* of the payment due?" She kept one eye on the office next door, watching for any sign of Austin. "The guy's a jerk. Maybe he shouldn't have had to pay his share of the bill, but everyone else gave us a good evaluation…" She broke off with a sound of frustration.

"I don't like this. The Judds have never had to resort to trickery to get what's theirs."

"There's nothing wrong with making a man work for

what he's already taken," she spouted back. "Besides, two weeks isn't nearly long enough to earn back what he owes us. It'll be a drop in the bucket."

"You're not doing this for the money, Kacy. You're doing it because you have a personal vendetta against the man."

"I do not!" she vehemently denied.

"Yes, you do."

"Does this mean you're not going to go along with me on this?"

There was a dead silence on the line.

"Dusty, you *have* to back me on this. I've already told Bill Cox Austin's a ranch hand we're hiring."

"Damn, Kacy, why didn't you talk to me about this before you started all of this?"

"Because I knew you'd tell me to call his people in Chicago and put him on a plane going home."

"Why didn't he leave with the others?"

"Who knows? His secretary said he was taking a two-week vacation. Maybe he wanted to spend it in North Dakota."

"You called his office?"

"Of course. You don't think I'd just hatch this scheme without covering the bases first, do you? We have two weeks…that's how long it'll be before anyone misses him."

"I can't believe I'm going to go along with this," he moaned.

The door to her grandfather's office opened. "I've gotta go. We'll be home in a little bit. Make sure you tell everyone, okay?"

"Kacy, I…"

At that moment Austin emerged. With a "bye," Kacy slammed the phone down. Then she said to Austin, "I just talked to my brother. He says you did fill out a written application, and he was impressed with your interview. You're welcome to work for us.''

''Then I guess I'm in your hands.'' He gave Kacy the most sincere, heartstopping smile she had ever seen.

She smiled back, but it was not a smile of benevolence. ''I guess you are.''

And so the deception began.

Chapter Eight

Kacy was surprised by what a bump on the head could do to a man. Gone was the arrogant, sarcastic Austin who had taunted her and looked down his nose at her. In his place was a courteous stranger who, despite having no memory of what had happened between the two of them, still had the power to keep her off balance with a simple look or gesture. That's what happened when he came around to her side of the truck and opened the door for her.

"Why'd you do that?" she asked, not expecting such attentiveness.

He shrugged. "It just seemed like the natural thing to do." He shoved his hands to his hips and shook his head. "This is really weird. I don't have a memory yet I know what kind of behavior is acceptable when a man is with a lady."

A lady. Not once since she'd met him had Austin treated her like a lady. Quite the opposite. Of course they hadn't exactly gotten off on the right foot, either. Not that it would have mattered. Austin Bennett was not the kind of man she wanted opening doors for her.

As he climbed into the pickup, he seemed to fill up more than his share of the cab. It was unsettling having him sit across from her. She forced herself to remember the last time they had been together in the truck. The sarcastic comments, the rude questions, the moose in the road...the memory brought a half smile to her face, prompting Austin to ask, "Am I amusing you?"

There was a hint of the old Austin in that question, but there was nothing in his face that led her to believe he was annoyed by her grin. "No. I was just thinking that life takes some unexpected twists, that's all."

She could feel his eyes on her face as she drove, but she refused to look in his direction. Instead, she slipped a cassette into the tape deck and listened to Reba McIntyre sing about a love gone wrong.

"You don't mind, do you?" she asked as Reba's voice filled the cab.

"No, it's all right." After a few minutes he asked, "Who is this singing?"

"Her name is Reba McIntyre. She sings country western."

"It's nice."

Kacy nearly chuckled. She couldn't imagine that Austin Bennett, the CEO, would have ever said that country western music was nice.

A silence stretched between them, one Kacy was in no hurry to break. She was relieved that he didn't want to talk. The Austin sitting beside her was not someone she wanted to get to know. All she wanted from him at this point was work—and a lot of it.

When they drove under the wrought iron arch with "Triple J" written across it, Kacy asked, "Does any of this look familiar to you?"

"No, should it?"

"Yeah. You've been here before."

"Did I see you when I was here?"

"Yes."

"I don't remember."

"None of it?"

"No." When she didn't continue the conversation he asked, "You do believe me, don't you?"

She glanced sideways at him. "Why wouldn't I?"

He sighed. "Because I'm having a hard time believing it myself."

Kacy had to admit that several times the thought had crossed her mind that maybe he wasn't telling the truth. There was something in the way he looked at her, as if he knew they had done more than talk to each other. Once a man had kissed a woman, there was something between them that time never erased. It was *that* look that had been in his eyes when he first saw her—or at least she thought it was. Now she wondered if it wasn't her guilty conscience seeing something that wasn't there.

He rubbed his forehead with his fingers. "My mind isn't empty. Far from it. I just can't remember being here before."

Kacy could hear the frustration in his voice. "Granddad's a good doctor. If he says your memory will come back, it'll come back."

"Hopefully soon. I don't want you to think I'm trying to take advantage of your hospitality."

She shrugged. "That thought never crossed my mind. Besides, it's not like you're staying at the ranch for free. You *are* going to be working for us."

"Maybe your brother will be able to tell me what he knows about my past. If I could remember one thing—anything—that would give me a clue as to who I am. For all I know I could be…well…anybody." His voice was tentative, so unlike the arrogant Austin Bennett.

"I suppose you could look at it as a chance to start over with a clean slate."

"You think I needed to erase what was on my slate?"

For just one moment she was tempted to tell him the truth. To let him know just how nasty he had been at the ranch. To tell him exactly what she thought about him not paying his bill. But then she glanced into those blue eyes and saw nothing but innocence. Since he didn't remember being at the ranch, it would do no good to yell at him for anything.

So she said, "I don't know you well enough to make that judgment."

"Yet you're willing to trust me."

"Trust you?"

"You're giving me a job without knowing very much about me. You're taking me in when I have literally nothing in my pockets, not one penny. Sounds to me like trust. And kindness," he added respectfully.

An icy blast of guilt chilled her bones. She worked hard at keeping her voice even as she said, "We need another pair of hands around the ranch. Just because you're going through some rough times doesn't mean we shouldn't hire you."

He turned to look out the rear window. "This feels so strange. I must have been down this road before, but I can't remember any of this." He faced the front again and squinted. "I should know where I'm going, where I've been. This is all so strange."

He was quiet for a few moments before saying, "I must have been looking for work if I applied for a job at a ranch." He sounded as if he were trying to convince himself, not her.

Instead of parking in her usual spot next to the lodge,

she pulled up alongside the bunkhouse. "This is it." She turned off the engine and hopped out of the truck.

Austin took his time getting out, looking at everything with wide eyes. She didn't miss how his gaze lingered on the lodge.

"We run a type of dude ranch here," she explained. "The lodge is where the guests sleep. The house over there is the original homestead—updated, of course."

He looked toward the two-story home with its tall columns and wide verandah. "Is that where you live?"

"No, I have my own place."

"You live alone?"

The look he gave her made her feel as if someone was rubbing velvet over her bare skin. Damn. Even with amnesia he oozed sexual tension. "No...I have two cats."

She unlocked the bunkhouse door and led him inside. "It's a little musty-smelling in here because all of the hired hands right now are local so no one's used this place for a while." She opened several windows. "You can take whichever bed you want. As you can see, there are foot lockers for your personal things."

"I won't need one, will I?" He spread his hands in a helpless gesture. "This is all I've got."

"We'll get you fixed up with some things. There's a small shop in the lobby that carries everything from toothpaste to blue jeans." She pushed open a door and flipped a light switch. "The bathroom's in here." He followed her into the small space and once again she had the feeling that he was too close for comfort. The way her body reacted to his nearness told her she'd be wise to avoid being in small spaces with him.

"You're responsible for your own housekeeping while you're here," she informed him, moving on to open a closet containing a broom, a mop and various cleansers.

He didn't protest, nor did he look happy about it. He just stared blankly.

"I'll get you some clean sheets so you can make up your bed. Mondays through Fridays everyone on the ranch eats in the main dining room in the lodge. On the weekends, we eat at the house. Since it's Friday and the guests have left, dinner this evening will be at the house."

He looked a bit overwhelmed and Kacy had to fight the sympathy that threatened to soften her attitude toward him.

"I'm going to have to take a shower and change my shirt before I do anything," he told her.

For the first time Kacy noticed the blood stains on the yellow shirt. She shivered. As much as she wanted to get even with Austin Bennett, she did care that the man had been hurt. He might even have been killed. Resolutely, she pushed the thought, and the resulting sympathy, from her mind.

"Then we should visit the shop first thing."

Déjà vu, Kacy thought. Only five days ago he had arrived without his luggage in search of something to wear. She remembered the disdain in his voice as she had showed him the western wear shop. He had scoffed at the notion of wearing boots, yet here he was, looking like a cowboy.

It puzzled her. Why would a man who hadn't wanted anything to do with ranch life, be wandering around North Dakota in blue jeans?

"What is this job I've applied for?"

"Ranch hand."

"As in riding a horse, rounding up cattle…that type of stuff?"

"Umm-hmm. Plus the usual—you know, mucking out the barns…"

"Mucking?"

"Yeah, as in hosing out the stalls, and all that…" She didn't go into much detail. He had plenty of time to find out what it meant to muck out the barn. It was a scene she was going to enjoy immensely.

There was a long silence followed by a sigh on his part. For just one moment when he looked at her she saw a lost little boy. She didn't want to let him affect her emotionally, but he did.

"You sound troubled," she remarked quietly.

"Frustrated would be a better word." He looked about the room with a critical eye. Although he didn't say anything, Kacy wondered if he wasn't thinking he was too good for the Spartan accommodations. "All I have right now is a name and the clothes on my back. It's a rather humbling position for any man to find himself in."

And one I want you to be in, she reminded herself. She needed to squash any sympathy for him with the memory of how he had behaved the past five days and with the fact that he owed her family. It was best to stay as detached from his situation as possible.

No, he needed no sympathy whatsoever. If her plan was going to work, she needed to remember that at all times. For a man like Austin Bennett, a slice of humble pie was just desserts.

"If you're concerned about money, we can advance you part of your wages until you get back on your feet." *A very small part,* she added silently to herself. "Actually, you look about the same size as my brother Mark.

He can probably loan you a few things and what you can't find in the shop you can probably pick up in town.''

Thinking of Mark made her realize that she needed to talk to the rest of the family. Dinner would be a good time. Which was why she said to Austin, "You know, you're looking a bit ragged around the edges. Maybe you don't want to eat with the rest of the family this evening. I could bring you a plate of dinner down here.''

Worry creased the lines of his forehead. "You're not changing your mind, are you?''

"About what?''

"About me staying here.''

She gave him a genuine smile. "There's no need for you to worry about that, Austin. I want you to work for us.''

"You won't be sorry. I'm a hard worker and I'll do a good job.''

"Oh, I'm sure you will.'' She paused at the door. "Now, would you like me to bring dinner here?''

"I *am* tired. Are you sure you wouldn't mind?''

"Not at all.''

"I DON'T SEE how you're going to pull this off,'' Mark stated over mashed potatoes and gravy that evening.

"It'll work,'' Kacy said confidently, not wanting to admit that now that she had actually set the plan in motion she was having second thoughts herself.

"You're just lucky Dad's out of town this week,'' Dusty chastised her. "What are you going to do if he returns and Austin's still here?''

"I'll tell him the truth. He'll understand.''

Both of her brothers snorted in disbelief. Then Mark said, "If you ask me, Dad's not going to be the problem.

Austin is. What are you going to do when he asks to see his job application?''

"I'll show it to him. I filled it out myself so I'm very familiar with it." She made a face at her brother, the one she used to pull when they were ten and eight and she wanted to have the upper hand.

"You made up a bogus job application?" Suzy looked at her with wide eyes.

"What about references? Did you make those up, too?" Mark asked.

"I used dead people."

"Dead people!" Suzy nearly choked on her iced tea.

"You know that guy that lived next to Uncle Ray in South Dakota? I put his name down. Plus Uncle Hank. This way if he tries to call them he'll get a recording that says the number's no longer in service," Kacy said confidently.

"More lying," Mark remarked with a sigh.

"It's not lying. It's doing what's necessary to get back some of the money that guy cheated us out of."

"That's like trying to right a wrong with another wrong," Suzy said righteously.

Kacy shot the younger woman a cross look. "I don't think you're the one to be worrying about telling little white lies—not after all those times you had me tell that guy from Rugby you were visiting Granddad when you were really out with Justin Doleman."

"All right, all right." Suzy held up her hands to stop the flow of words. "You made your point."

"Kacy, we want to get the money out of this guy just as much as you do," Dusty told her. "It's just that we're all a bit worried about the way you're going about getting it."

"Well, you don't need to be. I told you. I have it all figured out. I've covered every base," she assured him.

"What about his family in Chicago?" her sister-in-law Diane interjected. "Won't they be looking for him?"

"Got that covered, too," Kacy said proudly. "After he left here he apparently called his secretary and told her he was taking two weeks' vacation. No one expects him to show up before then."

"He must have made arrangements and left hotel numbers," Mark said logically.

"Uh-uh. His secretary told me she didn't know where he was—only that he was going out west to spend some time alone."

"Maybe that's what she's supposed to tell everybody," Mark cautioned.

That gave Kacy a moment. "No problem. I'll take care of it."

"How?"

Before she could answer Mark said, "Maybe it's better if we all don't know how she plans to do that."

That earned Mark a cross look as well. "I'll send a telegram just to make sure. Tell her he's doing one of those wilderness experiences and that he'll contact her when he gets back." She looked at the three dubious faces staring at her and insisted, "This is going to work."

By the looks on their faces, Kacy knew she was the only one who thought so. Then Suzy said, "What if one of the staff members recognizes him? I mean if he's working around the ranch he's bound to run into someone who saw him here before. And won't he be eating meals with everyone?"

That was something Kacy hadn't thought about. She

knew that when it came to her own family members, there wouldn't be a problem. But there was the possibility that one of the employees would see him and become curious as to why he was working at the ranch.

"I'll put him to work at my place."

That raised several sets of eyebrows and earned a few knowing glances.

"The shed needs to be moved."

"It's going to take more than one man to do that job," Dusty warned her.

"Then I'll have him build me that retaining wall I've been talking about."

"The guy probably doesn't have a clue as to how to build anything. He's a suit," Mark pointed out.

"What's so complicated about building a wall? He's not stupid, you know. If he can run some fancy furniture company he can certainly follow the instructions that come with the stone."

The laughter at the table told her what they thought of her statement.

"And there's grass to be mowed, and I've got those dead trees that went down in that last storm. They need to be taken down and cut up."

"You're going to trust that guy with a chain saw?" Mark's eyes widened.

"And you guys have been talking about hiring someone to get rid of all that lumber that's left over from when they built the house."

"What happens when he remembers who he really is?" Suzy asked.

Kacy shrugged. "I guess he'll go home. In the meantime we'll get as much work out of him as we can in exchange for his debt."

"He's going to expect a paycheck," Mark reminded her.

"So?"

"So how are we going to collect what he owes us when you're paying him wages?"

She took a moment to contemplate the situation. "I'll tell him payday is once a month."

Dusty made no bones about what he thought of her plan. "I don't like it. The Triple J has never had to resort to trickery to accomplish its goals."

"We've never been stiffed for this much money," Kacy reminded him. Then she scrunched up her napkin and tossed it beside the plate. "Look. You don't have to have anything to do with this. I'll take full responsibility for Austin's presence at the ranch. I have plenty of work he can do."

"Your own personal slave, eh?" Mark quipped.

"All I want to do is see that he works as hard as anyone else does on this ranch. You seem to think this is some sort of personal vendetta I have against the man."

"Isn't it?" Dusty was the one brave enough to ask.

"No. I'm just trying to get back some of the money he owes us. As I said, if he wasn't satisfied personally with our program, then he should have refused to pay his individual fee. But to stiff us for half the entire bill...well, that was downright nasty. You know what I think? I think he was more upset that he made a fool of himself on Old Yellow than he was with the program."

"I think it was the air conditioner that did him in," Mark contributed his thoughts. "Boy, was he spittin' mad. He called the switchboard thirteen times that last night he was here."

"He didn't like that fact that he couldn't get his Internet connection, either," Suzy pointed out. "He came up to the front desk and demanded to speak to someone at the local telephone company."

"He was like a fish out of water here. Guys like him should stay in the corporate zone," Dusty remarked.

"The second day he called all over trying to find a place to buy horehound drops. When he finally found a shop that had them he bribed one of the maids to drive the seventy-five miles to get them," Suzy added

"Figures a guy like that would eat horehound drops. What are they anyway?" Mark asked.

"He gave me one. It was a hard candy that tasted kinda bitter," Suzy answered.

"Whatever..." Kacy broke off, tired of talking about Austin Bennett. "What I need to know is if we have our stories straight."

The four heads nodded but Kacy wasn't convinced. "All right. Listen up. He was here a couple of days ago applying for a job, said he had to tie up a few loose ends, that he'd be back today."

Again, the heads nodded, the voices mumbled.

"Here's what we know about him. He's a wanderer. No next of kin listed on the application, originally from Iowa."

"Iowa? Why can't he be from Illinois? It'd be less confusing."

"Since the law prohibits us from asking personal details on a job application, we don't need to know very much about him. Just his work experiences. And those are covered. The previous employers are dead." Kacy grinned impishly. "I figure the only other person I need to let in on this is DJ. Chances are Austin will run into him at some time during his stay."

"What if this backfires on us?" Suzy wanted to know.

"What if?" Kacy retorted sassily. "Nobody's forcing him to stay here against his will."

Dusty rubbed his five o'clock stubble. "I don't know."

"Do you really want to let this guy go back to Chicago when he owes us all that money?"

"She has a point, Dusty," Mark came to her support, surprising Kacy.

"Granddad says the amnesia could last two days or two months. The way I look at it is this. Austin's a businessman. If he had the opportunity to recover lost income, don't you think he'd do it?"

"After the hard time he gave everyone around here, it would be kinda fun to see him ankle-deep in manure," Mark admitted.

"So are we in agreement? No one says anything until he remembers on his own?"

Reluctantly, they all agreed.

"Trust me. This is going to work," Kacy assured them.

She only wished she felt as confident as her words sounded.

BY THE END OF the weekend, Austin had done just about every disgusting job around the ranch Kacy could think of for him to do. She figured he had shoveled more manure in those two days than he had seen in his entire lifetime. Not once had he complained.

Bright and early Monday morning before the guests were up, she took him into the kitchen where DJ was already at work on breakfast. Then with a thermos of lemonade and a box lunch in his hand, she led him to the pickup with the news that he would be working on the south end of the ranch today.

Once again, they didn't talk while they were in the truck. Austin hadn't said much of anything since he'd been at the ranch. She didn't understand why. If she were the one with amnesia, she figured she'd be asking questions left and right. He didn't. He was like an obedient child. Doing exactly as he was told, asking no questions, keeping quiet.

"We're here," she announced as her white cottage came into view.

She parked the truck to the side of the house and climbed out. "Follow me," she instructed as he joined her and started walking toward the back of the house.

"This must be your place," he remarked.

"What makes you say that?"

He shrugged. "It looks like the kind of house you'd live in, that's all."

It was better than a compliment on her own appearance. Kacy had sat down with an architect and designed the house herself, wanting it to be a reflection of who she was. That's why it had lots of windows to let in the sun, including two skylights that allowed her to soak in her claw-footed tub and watch the stars at night.

"It's a nice place," he added, when she didn't say anything.

"Thank you, although you might be cursing it by the time the day's over."

He looked puzzled. "Why do you say that?"

"Come. I'll show you." She led him around to the back of the house to the pile of debris littering the ground. "This needs to be gone."

He grimaced as if he suddenly realized the implication. "And you want me to get rid of it."

She nodded. "Anything that won't burn has to go in that Dumpster over there." She pointed to a large green metal bin sitting about one hundred feet away. "The rest has to be moved to that clearing over there." She swung her arm in the opposite direction. "That's where we'll have a big old bonfire. But we can't do it here because it's too close to the house."

"Isn't there a piece of equipment that could do this?"

"Yeah, it's called a pair of hands," she drawled sarcastically. She expected him to come back with his own bit of sarcasm. He didn't. He laughed.

She led him to the barn-shaped garden shed. "Any tools you might need are in here." She flung the door open to reveal rakes, shovels and other implements. She wondered how many looked familiar to him. Even without the amnesia she doubted whether Austin Bennett knew what to do with half of them.

She pointed to another small building whose paint was faded. "That is a hunting cabin. There's a pump and sink inside and an outhouse out back."

"An outhouse?" She could see the idea was a distasteful one to him.

"The cowboys around here don't care about modern facilities," she remarked, "But if you want to use the bathroom in my house, I guess it's all right." She quickly changed the subject, feeling oddly embarrassed. "If you get tired of hauling that rubbish, there's a chainsaw in the shed. See those trees?" She pointed to a row of elms that had been uprooted during a recent storm. "They need to come down."

"Anything else?"

She raised one eyebrow. "I'd like a path cleared to the river."

"There's a river?"

"Hmm-mmm. You just can't see it because the brush is so thick." She walked over to the dense green vegetation and said, "I'd like to be able to see the river from my porch."

He nodded, then said, "So what should have priority? The trees?"

She thought for a moment before answering, trying to decide which would create the most strenuous work. "It probably would be a good idea to get those dead trees cut up."

"I'll see to it," was all he said.

As she walked back toward her truck, he followed her. Before she climbed inside, she said, "I'll be back later this afternoon. Do you have any questions?"

"Just one." He waited until she was inside, then leaned his forearms on the door of the pickup and asked her, "Do you think I'm really a cowboy?"

Startled, she asked, "What makes you ask that?"

He shoved his hands out in front of her. "Look at the blisters I have from shoveling the past couple of days. If I was used to working with my hands, they'd be toughened up."

"Maybe you haven't been working as a ranch hand lately. You told Dusty you had loose ends to tie up. It could be that you had another job."

He didn't look convinced. "That isn't the only thing. When you mentioned using the outdoors to...well, you know...that sounded like something I wouldn't do. It only stands to reason that cowboys being out on the range often must relieve themselves in such a manner, but to me...well, it doesn't seem right."

Kacy hoped he couldn't see the guilt she felt in her heart. "Do you hate the work you've been doing at the ranch?"

"No, I'm not complaining about the work. It's just that it doesn't feel natural to me."

"Does anything feel natural to you?"

"It feels natural talking to you." He smiled then, a very charming smile that made her feel like she was sixteen years old and watching Bobby Jo Martin tip his hat at her after he had ridden the meanest bull in the high school rodeo.

As Kacy drove away, she thought again about the opportunity fate had given her. Not only had the amnesia given her a chance to collect on a debt. It had given her and Austin another chance, too. They could put aside any baggage that had cluttered up their relationship in the past and start over with a fresh slate.

That thought had a tiny smile tugging at her lips all the way home.

Chapter Nine

For the remainder of the morning, Kacy couldn't stop thinking about Austin. Putting him to work at her place had seemed like a good idea, but now that he was alone on her property, she was having second thoughts about the wisdom of her plan. She didn't want him wandering through her house and she wished she hadn't left her door unlocked. But until today, there had never been any reason to lock up the place.

Nor was there any reason to think Austin would go inside. He had the hunting cabin to use if he needed water.

Still thinking about it after lunch, she decided it would be wise to check up on him. She hopped in the pickup and drove home, but instead of parking outside the house, she left the truck at the end of the gravel road. She wanted to see just what kind of a worker Austin Bennett really was when there was no one watching him.

As she walked toward the house, she heard nothing except an occasional chirping of a bird. No chain saw splitting trees. No wood being clanged against the side of the Dumpster. No hedge clippers clearing the brush.

That's because Austin wasn't at work. When she reached the backyard she saw that a couple of trees had been sawed up and the wood neatly stacked in a pile, but the chain saw sat idle. Austin was nowhere in sight.

Kacy walked over to the hunting shack, calling out tentatively as she entered the small wooden building. She pushed the door open and stuck her head inside. "Austin?"

There was no answer. "Austin, are you in here?" she repeated a bit louder.

It didn't take long to discover the building was vacant.

She went back outside and glanced toward the house. Surely he hadn't gone inside? The hairs on the back of her neck stood on end. Would he be so bold as to pry into her living quarters?

She hurried up the back steps and pushed the door open. Normally she would have left her boots in the mudroom, but not today. She stomped through every room on the first floor calling out his name. To her relief, he was in none of them.

She took the stairs two at a time only to discover he wasn't in her sanctuary, either. Her art studio was empty. She exhaled a long sigh and went back down the stairs.

As she walked back outside, she knew that there was only one place he could be. At the river. Thanks to years of use, a narrow path led from the hunting cabin to the river's edge. Kacy followed the dirt trail to its end and found Austin.

He was swimming. Frolicking would have been a better word. He looked like a gleeful little kid at play. The pile of clothes on the bank of the river told Kacy he wasn't wearing anything—not even his boxers. That should have set off an alarm in Kacy's head. It didn't.

That's because Austin Bennett, naked in the water, fascinated her. Alone and thinking there was no one to see him, he acted like he was twelve years old, bringing an understanding smile to Kacy's face. There was nothing like a skinny-dip in the river to bring out the child in anyone.

Before he saw her, she slipped behind a thicket of scrub brush. She pushed a branch aside until she had a view of him in the water just as he dove beneath the surface only to rise again like some sort of Greek god.

In the deepest part of the river, the water was up to his chest. How long Kacy stood there peeping at him she didn't know. As his playful swim came to an end, he waded toward shore. With each step he took, the water covered less and less of his body. Kacy knew she should leave—or at least turn away. In a few seconds she would see *all* of Austin Bennett.

Unfortunately, it was that very thought that kept her glued to her spot behind the brush. She felt as if she were fifteen and peeping through the narrow crack in the wall of the boys' locker room at school. Her mouth went dry, her pulse raced and a funny tingling invaded her entire body. Only Austin Bennett was nothing like the boys in her ninth grade gym class. Even though he didn't have the finely buffed body of a health club regular, he was still a splendid specimen of the male species and she was standing there staring at him, practically with her tongue hanging out.

She clamped her mouth shut by biting on her upper lip. It wasn't as though she had never seen a naked man before. Only the men she had seen looked nothing like this. As Austin used his shirt to soak up the glistening droplets of water on his skin, Kacy watched in total fascination. It was only as he started to get dressed that she realized what she was doing.

She squeezed her eyes shut and turned away, wondering how she could have stood there for so long admiring a naked man. As quietly as possible, avoiding branches and twigs, she scampered up the embankment and back to the drive. Once she reached the gravel road she ran all the way to the pickup.

Panting, she hopped inside and rested her head against the steering wheel. As soon as she had regained her composure, she started the truck and drove back to the ranch. All the way home her cheeks flamed. Finally, she turned on the air-conditioning. But she knew that it was a futile effort. Nothing short of a cold shower was going to cool her down.

IF KACY COULD have sent one of her brothers to pick up Austin and return him to the ranch that evening, she would have done it. Despite all of her begging for one of them to do the deed for her, however, they both refused, saying this was her plan and she was the one who was going to see it through.

She knew it would be wise to keep Austin away from the home place as much as possible. There would be less chance of anyone recognizing him that way. Plus, she wanted him to put in a twelve-hour day. After all, he was the one who had bragged about working twelve-, fourteen- and even sixteen-hour days.

Not chopping wood, a little voice reminded her. Answering that little voice out loud Kacy said, "Physical labor is good for him." Not that it mattered. He owed her and she was going to get payment, one way or the other.

As it turned out, one of the trail horses required the vet's attention and she had no choice but to wait until he had been to see the animal before going back to pick up Austin. By the time she returned to her cottage, all of the ranch guests had eaten and the sun was sinking into the horizon. She half expected Austin to be sitting on the lawn swing waiting for her to show up. He wasn't. He was out back, stacking sawed up pieces of tree trunks into neat piles in the exact spot she'd told him to put them.

He was bare-chested, reminding Kacy that he had used his shirt as a towel earlier that day. The memory of the scene at the river caused her whole body to warm and she rubbed the moist palms of her hands down the legs of her jeans.

Although it was evening, the air hadn't cooled at all. Sultry, was the word that came to Kacy's mind. It was the kind of day that made muscles gleam with sweat and hair curl into unmanageable coils. One look at Austin told her that the heat and humidity had caused both to happen to him. Kacy's heart took a funny beat. He looked nothing like the suit who had arrived only a week ago.

When he finally noticed her appearance, she found herself apologizing. "I'm sorry I'm so late. One of the horses has a bad foot and I had to wait for the vet to come."

He shrugged off her apology. "What time *is* it anyway?"

"Almost eight-thirty." Her answer made her aware of just how long she had made him work. "Don't you have a watch?"

He shook his head. "Must have been stolen with the rest of my things."

That came as no surprise to Kacy. She had seen the gold Rolex watch he wore on his wrist and knew that it had to have cost thousands of dollars. No thief would have left it behind.

"You got a lot done today," she commented, looking at the pile of wood rather than his glistening biceps.

He grimaced as he rotated his shoulder, working it as if it were troubling him. "They were big trees."

It should have made her happy that he was obviously feeling aches and pains from the work he had done. It didn't. The sight of that bare chest wouldn't let her feel any antipathy toward him at all.

"I'm afraid you missed dinner at the lodge so I had to box you up something...again." She held up one of the two plastic containers she carried in her hands.

"That's fine," he told her. "It's probably better if I eat by myself. I'm not very good company."

At one time she would have agreed with him, but now she wasn't as sure. "It can't be easy talking to people when you can't remember anything."

"That could be the reason. Or maybe I just don't like being around people. I mean, I really don't know, do I?" He dusted his hands off on his jeans and reached for his shirt which was dangling from one of the branches of a fallen tree.

His words were said with such genuine uncertainty that Kacy couldn't prevent the ripples of sympathy tugging on her heart. "I'm sure things will become clear eventually."

He didn't look convinced. He slipped his arms through the shirt sleeves, but didn't button the front. Kacy wondered if he was aware of how sexy he looked with it open. Obviously he wasn't. He reached for the plastic container. "Thanks for the dinner. I'll take it with me."

"Maybe you should eat it here," she heard herself say, much to her own surprise. "It's not going to stay warm for long."

He looked at her as if he hadn't heard correctly. "You want me to eat here?"

"Yes—unless you'd rather be by yourself."

"No, it's just..." He studied her face with a curiosity that had Kacy blushing, much to her chagrin. She was not one to blush every time a man showed interest in her.

"I'll set the table while you wash up," she told him, avoiding his eyes.

He didn't say another word, but headed for the hunting cabin.

While he was gone Kacy set two places at the picnic table on her porch. She pulled a can of frozen concentrated lemonade from the freezer and mixed it up in a glass pitcher. By the time he returned, she had filled two tall glasses with ice cubes and set them beside the bright red plates.

He waited for her to sit before he shoved his legs over the bench and sat across from her. When his stomach growled, he looked a bit embarrassed.

"You must be hungry," Kacy remarked.

"I am."

And not just for food, she realized. One didn't reach the age of twenty-six and not be able to recognize what that look meant in a man's eyes. Austin's eyes gleamed whenever they looked in her direction, which somehow excited and annoyed her at the same time.

She should have given him the boxed meal and sent him home. Having dinner with this man was not part of her plan. Nor was being attracted to him. But she was doing both.

"Umm. Smells like coq au vin," he said as he was about to open the container.

"It is. Our chef likes to serve fancy food to all the city slickers who come to the ranch."

He took a few more bites before he said, "This is really strange. How can I know which foods I like and dislike, yet I can't remember what happened three days ago?"

She shrugged. "I guess that's the way amnesia is. What else do you like?"

"Steak rare, baked potatoes no sour cream, coleslaw, escargots, coquilles St. Jacques."

"Coquilles St. Jacques? You must have eaten in some pretty fancy restaurants. Most of the folks I know would say barbecued ribs, burgers and fries…that kind of stuff."

He paused with his fork in midair. "Maybe I'm not a cowboy."

She shifted uneasily. "Of course there always is that possibility. We get a lot of cowboy wanna-bes around these parts. You know, guys who decide to give up the city life and see what it's like to rope steers, break horses and ride like the wind."

"Is that why you have me cutting up trees instead of working the cattle? Because you think I might only be a wanna-be cowboy?"

She didn't like the way his eyes seemed to see right inside her. She turned her attention to her plate. "I have you working here because I need the work done."

"And that's the only reason?"

"Sure." She lifted the glass pitcher and asked, "Lemonade? Or would you prefer water?"

"Lemonade's fine. Here, let me." He took the pitcher from her hand and filled both of their glasses. "You have a nice place."

"You went inside?"

"You don't need to look so startled. No, I didn't go into your home." His voice took on a defensive quality that almost reminded her of the arrogance Austin Bennett had often shown. "I wouldn't do that. All I meant is that it's a nice setting."

"Yes, it is. Thank you."

"Are there fish in the river?" The question managed to get rid of the bit of tension that clogged the air.

"Umm-hmm. Do you like to fish?"

He shrugged. "I don't know…maybe. I know I like to swim."

That caused Kacy's body to warm all over and she quickly looked away, hoping he wouldn't see anything on her face that would give him the slightest hint that she had seen him in the river. "That hunting cabin has seen its share of hunters and fishermen. Over the years it's been used as a rite of passage. Once you were old enough to spend the night there by yourself, you earned the right to strut around like a big shot…sort of a coming of age thing for the guys."

"What about the girls?"

"It's always been off limits to the women in the family."

"Is that why you built your house next to it?"

Again she shifted uncomfortably. Was she that obvious or was he simply perceptive at reading people? "You think I'm a rebel?"

"Are you?"

"No," she denied curtly, then took a drink of lemonade. "I just don't like being told I can't do something."

He grinned, as if he had just been let in on a big secret. "So tell me how you convinced your father to let you stay overnight by yourself."

"What makes you think I did?"

"You don't strike me as the kind of woman who gets left out of anything."

That compliment sent another rush of warmth through her. The guy was flirting with her and as much as she hated to admit it, she liked it.

"He didn't know I was out here," she confessed. "I said I was spending the night at my girlfriend's house and she told her parents she was spending the night at mine. Then we came here carrying a gunnysack with a couple of cans of pop, several bags of candy, a couple of flashlights and some playing cards. I also packed my favorite book."

"Which was?"

"*Black Beauty.* You remember reading it as a kid?"

"No." He took a drink of lemonade, then said, "I know the title just like I know that a plate is used for food and that we eat with a fork. I don't lack knowledge, Kacy, just memory."

"Isn't knowledge in your memory?"

He sighed and shoved his half-eaten plate aside. "According to your grandfather, there are different kinds of amnesia. I have what's called retrograde amnesia. I can't remember events that happened prior to my head injury, but I still can recall knowledge."

"My grandfather's a good doctor."

"I believe you," he told her, which made her realize that she had sounded defensive. "If he's right about my amnesia, my memory's not going to come back all at once, but in little pieces."

Which would be better for me, Kacy thought. "And have you noticed any bits returning?" She held her breath as she waited for his answer.

"Not yet."

She moaned as if in understanding, but it was really a sound of relief.

He changed the subject. "So you haven't told me whether or not you made it through that night in the hunting shack when it was just you and your girlfriend."

She sighed wistfully. "Everything was going great. I managed to get out of the house without my parents noticing I was gone. I didn't get lost riding over here even though it was really dark and there was no moonlight." She paused to smile at the memory. "It was so neat being all alone in the cabin. I felt as if I had passed a great test."

"Did you?"

"Not exactly. We had an unexpected visitor. A bear. Or at least we thought it was a bear."

"Let me guess. Dusty or Mark?"

"Both. If we hadn't been half-asleep, we would have realized it was them. But I woke up when Shannon screamed. She said she heard something growling. I told her she was just being a baby, but then the door was pushed open and in came this...this...this creature. It crawled around the cabin making this horrible noise. It only took the two of us about five seconds to fly out of that shack and head for home."

"I wouldn't think that you would scare very easily," he said with admiration.

"Normally I don't. Of course it didn't help that Shannon became hysterical." She shook her head at the memory. "We had to sleep in the barn because we had told our parents we were sleeping at each other's houses."

"You didn't know it was your brothers?"

"Not until the next morning. When I walked into the house, Dusty had this big old bearskin spread out on the floor. Mark giggled and told me our dad had found it at an auction sale and thought it would look good on the floor of the den. One look at the smart-aleck grins on their faces was all it took to know that they had been the ones crawling around and growling at us the night before.''

Austin grinned and again Kacy's heart flip-flopped. There was such a genuine look of interest in his face that she felt herself softening toward him. This Austin Bennett was so easy to talk to, so attentive to her every word…how could she not respond to him?

''So how did you get even?'' he asked.

''What makes you think I got even?''

''Didn't you?''

''No!''

''You didn't.'' Skepticism laced his words.

''No,'' she repeated.

She could feel his eyes on her face, studying it intently as if he could see whether or not she was telling the truth. She tried not to be self-conscious, but she was.

''You don't believe me, do you?'' she accused.

''Seeing you work around this ranch the past few days, I find it hard to believe that you would let anyone get the better of you, Kacy.''

It was said not critically, but with admiration. She felt herself warm again. ''All right. So I did play a little joke of my own. I mean, after all, that was downright nasty of them to pull such a trick on me. They knew that if I told Dad, I'd be the one who got the punishment for using the men's fishing cabin, not them.''

His eyes sparkled with curiosity. ''So tell me. What did you do?''

''I made them lunch,'' she said innocently.

''Uh-oh. Do I dare ask what you gave them for lunch?''

She hid a smile. "Well, let's just say they spent a lot of time in the bathroom that afternoon."

He grimaced. "Remind me never to get on your bad side."

It's too late for that, Kacy thought. But she wanted no reminders of why Austin was having dinner with her. She wanted their easy conversation to continue. That's why she asked with a sly smile, "So. How's your food?"

Before he took another bite of the chicken, he feigned concern as he asked, "You didn't cook this, did you?"

"No, as I said, we have a chef at the ranch."

"And a very good one." He savored a taste.

"I think so. I know we've had very few complaints over the years."

He seemed to relish each bite he took, so much so that again Kacy felt a twinge of guilt. He was probably starving. The lunch cook had made up for him hadn't exactly been hearty.

When he had finished, he said, "I bet you're a good cook."

"Why would you think that?"

"Because you appear to be a woman who's good at everything she does."

It sounded like an innocent compliment, but the look in his eyes made it much more. She found herself responding in a flirtatious manner. "I *am* good at just about everything I do. If I'm not good at it, I don't do it."

Admiration sparkled in his eyes. "You have a way with horses, that's for sure."

The compliment warmed her. She didn't want it to, but it did. "Thanks."

They continued to talk, mainly about what it was like

to grow up on a ranch in North Dakota. There was no sarcasm on Austin's part, no mockery, just a genuine interest in her recollections. Kacy was discovering that she liked the Austin Bennett without a memory and didn't understand why he was so different from the CEO who had visited the ranch.

Throughout dinner she couldn't help but notice that his hands were red and roughened. "Excuse me a minute, Austin. I want to get something for you."

She went into the house and headed straight for her bedroom where she found what she was looking for. A round jar with splotches of black on white. She took it with her and returned to the porch.

She set the jar down beside his plate. "Here. Use this. It'll help those hands feel better."

He read the label before opening the jar. "Apply to the udder after each milking...for teat cracks...this is for cows!" He looked at her, eyes wide.

"Humans use it, too," she assured him. "It's wonderful stuff. Just smooth some on and you'll see what I mean."

He hesitated, his face wrinkling in uncertainty.

"Really. I'm serious. They sell it in the drugstore with all the skin creams."

From the look on his face she could see that he still had his doubts, but he did as instructed, rubbing it into his hands. "Feels good," he said with a note of surprise.

"I told you it would. There are leather work gloves in the shed. You're welcome to use them tomorrow."

"Tomorrow?"

He didn't look overjoyed at the prospect. "You'll probably work here the rest of the week. Is that a problem?"

He shrugged. "Not at all. I thought I was going to be working with the cattle, that's all."

"Maybe next week."

Again, he simply shrugged in acquiescence.

When she began to clear the table, he jumped up to help her. "It's all right. I can take care of these," she insisted.

He held the screen door open for her, but didn't follow her inside. From where she stood in the kitchen rinsing off the plates, she could see him standing on the porch. Even with his back to her she felt a tremor of excitement at the sight of his tall figure leaning against her railing.

As an arrogant CEO she had found him attractive, appealing in a purely physical way. But now, as a cowboy with no memory...he was tugging on emotions she didn't want to let him near. And if there was one thing she didn't need it was to become emotionally involved with the man from whom she was looking for retribution.

She needed to get him back to the ranch. Off her property and away from her home. She quickly disposed of the dishes, then grabbed her keys and headed back outside, flipping on the porch light on her way.

"Okay. Let's go. I'll take you back to the ranch now," she said in a much sharper tone than she intended.

He didn't protest, but followed her down the porch steps and over to the pickup. Once more he opened her truck door for her and all the way home he was quiet, which suited Kacy just fine. The more Austin spoke, the less anger she harbored. And she needed to be angry with him. After all, he owed her family a lot of money. She needed to keep that at the forefront of her thoughts at all time.

When they arrived at the bunkhouse, he hopped out

of the truck before Kacy had brought the vehicle to a complete stop. "Same time tomorrow?" he asked before slamming the door shut.

"Sure. See you then."

And without another word, Austin Bennett walked away. And all Kacy could think about was how nice it was to have had his company for dinner.

BY THE END OF his first week at the Judd ranch, Austin was no closer to figuring out who he was than he had been the day he arrived. Each day had passed in the same way. Kacy came to get him at sunrise, he worked at her place until sundown, they ate dinner together, then she took him back to the ranch.

It was a routine that Austin liked—especially the part about eating dinner with Kacy Judd. The more he saw of her, the more he wanted to be with her. He may have forgotten his life before arriving at the ranch, but amnesia hadn't stopped him from feeling attracted to a woman.

And he was definitely attracted to Kacy Judd. Every time he saw her his body reacted to her presence in a way no man ever forgets. She was strong-willed, feisty, accustomed to getting her own way and definitely not a woman who was going to sit back and let a man do the talking for her. That's what he liked about her.

He knew that beneath that rough and dusty exterior was one soft woman. A woman who was just as aware of him as he was of her. It was there in her eyes when she looked at him. She wanted him as much as he wanted her.

The problem was, who was the man she wanted? He figured it was that unanswered question that kept her as skittish as the newborn filly in her pasture. Whenever they were alone together, she displayed a caution in her attitude he knew could only be attributed to his circumstances. During the past week he had proven to her that he wasn't a man she needed to treat with suspicion. And he thought that she was relaxing a bit more each night when they ate dinner together.

He suspected she didn't trust him around the ranch guests. That had to be the reason why she found work for him at her place and why they ate dinner there, as well. On Friday she surprised him by showing up several hours earlier than usual.

"You're early," he stated the obvious.

"I thought you'd appreciate quitting early. But we don't have to eat now. It's cold cuts and salad," she told him.

"Then put them in the refrigerator and let's go for a swim."

She looked stupefied. She stood there, mouth open, speechless. What had happened to the feisty redhead who always had a quick comeback for everything he said?

"I'm not sure that's good idea."

"Why not?"

"The river's not the safest place to swim," she told him, but he knew that wasn't the real reason for her hesitancy.

"Aw, come on. A woman who rides the way you do isn't going to worry about a tiny stream of water, are you?" As he spoke he undid the belt around his waist, amused by the way her eyes widened. Within a matter of seconds he had dropped his pants, revealing a pair of black tight swimming trunks. The look on her face was priceless.

"Where did you get those?" she demanded, her cheeks still tinged with pink.

"Suzy left them on my cot with a note attached saying I might need them."

"They look kind of silly with cowboy boots," she said, recovering her sense of humor.

"I'll take the boots off if you'll go in the water with me. Is it a deal? Or do you want a guy painting your shed wearing nothing but cowboy boots and Speedos?"

She laughed then. "All right. It's a deal. I'll put this stuff away and get changed."

He watched her walk toward the house and was grateful she had turned her back to him, for the swaying of those hips caused a reaction the fabric of the Speedos wouldn't hide. Just before she reached the house he called out, "Hey—I'll meet you in the water."

She didn't turn around, but waved her hat in the air in acknowledgment. Austin finished undressing, then hurried toward the river. He hit the water with a splash, grateful for its refreshing coolness.

It wasn't long before Kacy appeared on the path to the river. Austin knew he had been smart to get in the water. He needed something to tamp the heat that spread over his body at the sight of her. She wore a lime green one-piece swimsuit that told him what he had suspected all along—that she had a figure that would make any man's heart beat faster. Over her shoulders were slung two thick white towels.

"I brought you a towel," she called out to him before kicking off her sandals and wading into the water. She let out a tiny, shrill sound as she inched her way in.

Unable to resist the temptation, Austin splashed water at her. She shrieked and splashed back, which started a water fight between the two of them that ended with each seeking escape beneath the water. When they surfaced, they were both laughing.

"Whew! That really cools one off, doesn't it?" she proclaimed, squeezing the water from her hair as she pushed it back from her face. "I can't remember the last time I swam here."

"Don't you really use this for swimming?" he asked, looking out at the gently flowing river.

"When we were kids we did, but now that we have the pool..." she trailed off.

He looked at her and suddenly an image of her wearing soaking wet clothing and looking every bit as desirable as she did now flashed in his mind. He closed his eyes briefly and saw himself kissing her. Just as quickly as the image came, it left.

"What's wrong?" she asked.

"Nothing. I just had this memory—or maybe it wasn't a memory. Maybe it was a wish." He rubbed his temples with his fingertips.

"Tell me about it," she urged, moving closer to him.

That was all the invitation he needed. He didn't tell her a thing, but pulled her into his arms and kissed her. It was every bit as wonderful as he had imagined, and then some. She was soft in his arms, yet fiery in her response to his mouth on hers.

Without hesitation, her lips opened to his tongue, allowing him to taste her sweetness. Despite being in a stream of cold water, heat spread through every part of him, creating a pulsating that urged him to hold tight to her trembling figure.

He could feel her fingers twining themselves in the wet hair at the back of his neck, her supple breasts pressing into his bare chest, tantalizing him. The kiss intensified as his tongue thrust deeper into her mouth, producing a soft whimper of delight that also had her moving against him in a seductive motion.

When the kiss finally ended, she leaned against him, the slowly moving water gently lapping against their entangled bodies.

"What was that for?" she asked, her eyes darkened with desire.

Again he had a sense of déjà vu, as though she had asked him that on another occasion, which was absurd, since he had only been at the ranch to apply for a job. Why would he have kissed her, unless...

"Did we know each other before I came to apply for a job here?" he asked.

"No. Why do you ask?"

"Because when I kissed you just now it felt as if it were the most natural thing in the world, like I had done it before and you had asked me that same question—why?" He took her mouth once more, but this time only to briefly taste the sweetness. When he pulled away, she looked disappointed and he had to fight with all of his willpower not to kiss her again.

But she made no attempt to pull him back to her. Instead she said, "We'd better get out of here before the mosquitoes start to bite."

"What happened between us just now...it was special, right?" He hated to even have to ask the question, but he needed to know. Although he had no memory of kissing any women, he knew instinctively that it couldn't have been like this with anyone else.

She moistened her lips before answering. "Are you asking me if I kiss other men like that and if it's the same?"

"Is it?"

Again she hesitated, looked away, then finally stared into his eyes and said, ''No. It was definitely special.''

''Good, because for the first time since I lost my memory I finally feel as if something is going right in my life.''

To his surprise, she didn't smile and say that she was happy. She pushed herself away from him saying, ''We need to get out.'' And without another word she waded toward the riverbank.

Austin felt as if someone had tied a brick to his foot and challenged him in a race to the shore.

Chapter Ten

One week had passed without Austin recovering any memories. The bits and pieces Kacy's grandfather had predicted would occur never happened. Kacy saw it as a sign—an affirmation of what she was doing.

Actually, she didn't think the week could have gone much better. She had managed to keep Austin away from the ranch's other employees, eliminating the worry that anyone might recognize him. He had worked almost seventy long, hard hours of physical labor which was a good start at repaying the debt he owed her family. Since he hadn't regained any of his memory loss, he didn't have a clue as to why he was really at the ranch.

Overall, it had been a good week. Kacy's strategy for making Austin Bennett pay was going much better than even she had expected. There was only one small wrinkle in her plan.

Her conscience.

No matter how hard she tried to tell herself that keeping Austin at the ranch was justified by his previous behavior as a guest, she couldn't prevent the frequent attacks of guilt. Each time they occurred she managed to push them aside with a few reminders of just how nasty Austin had been during the week he had been in the program, but with each passing day, those memories faded and it became more difficult to defend her actions.

It didn't help that Austin did every assigned chore without so much as a word of protest. Or that he worked harder than any other employee at the ranch. Or that he asked for nothing and continually expressed his gratitude for her kindness in giving him a job and a place to stay when she knew nothing about his background.

And then there was the way her body reacted every time she saw him. Kacy had always thought there was no greater high than winning a barrel racing championship, but even that couldn't compare to the rush of adrenaline she experienced around him. It was as if every nerve in her body screamed out, "Attractive man in the vicinity!"

He was attractive. Actually, he was more than attractive. He was downright irresistible. This new Austin had a charming vulnerability that made her forget that he had ever uttered a sarcastic word to her or that he had treated her with disdain. That's because he was nothing like the CEO Austin.

Kacy knew it was pointless to deny that there was something sexual between them. She knew that he wanted her just as much as she wanted him. Call it chemistry or call it infatuation; there was no reason to pretend it didn't exist.

She didn't want to think about it. What she needed to do was learn how to deal with it. There was a physical connection between them. That's all it was. And why shouldn't there be? He was good-looking, sexy and at her command. Any woman in her boots would feel the same way.

On Sunday morning at breakfast Dusty made a suggestion that Kacy herself had been thinking. "Isn't it about time Austin gets a day off?" he asked.

Before Kacy could second the idea Austin said, "I'd rather not take any time off if you don't mind."

"Why not?" Kacy couldn't resist asking.

"Because I haven't finished painting the shed out back of your place and I like to see projects through to a finish." A smile gradually spread across his face—a wonderful, warm smile that had Kacy's heartbeat accelerating. "I guess that's something I just learned about myself. I'm a finisher."

"You're also a darn good worker," Dusty remarked, giving his sister a sharp look.

"He is and that's why I'm going to insist that he takes today off," Kacy injected.

"To do what?" Austin looked bemused. "I don't have any place to go, any people to see."

"That doesn't mean you shouldn't have some fun," she answered. "You're probably tired of seeing nothing but this ranch. I'll take you away for a while."

That raised a few eyebrows among the family. Kacy shot each of them a warning look.

"Are you sure you don't want me to finish painting the shed?" Austin asked.

"Uh-uh. That can wait until tomorrow. Sunday's a day to rest."

"But I can finish in a couple of hours," he protested.

"Then tomorrow morning it'll be done," Kacy assured him.

Austin was not about to be sidetracked. "Tomorrow I planned to start on that retaining wall you want down by the river."

That brought Dusty into their conversation. "I thought

I told you to wait until I could give you a couple of guys before you started that project."

"Austin says he can do it." She noticed how her brother's eyebrow was cocked in a familiar way. He was wondering what was going on between the two of them.

"That's an awful lot of work for one man." Mark's comment was directed at Kacy and meant to be critical.

"Is it?" she asked innocently.

"I don't mind," Austin told them. "Kacy would like to get the thing done and as long as you don't need me elsewhere on the ranch, I might as well do it."

"Let me get this straight." Dusty folded his arms across his chest and leaned back in his chair. "Are you saying you'd rather build a retaining wall rather than herd cattle?"

"I've been here a week and I've yet to sit on a horse," he pointed out.

Kacy and Dusty exchanged glances. "Did you want to ride?" she asked.

He looked uncomfortable with the question. "I'm not sure I should."

"Why? If you're worried that you don't have your own horse, it's not a problem. We have plenty of mounts," Mark pointed out.

"That's not it."

Kacy gave him a puzzled look. "Then what is it?"

He looked as if he didn't want to tell her, then finally said, "You teach riding, right?" When she nodded he went on, "Then you probably can tell by the way someone sits in a saddle whether or not he's experienced."

Suddenly Kacy understood the reason for his question. He wasn't sure if he could remember how to ride.

"Austin, are you worried that you don't know how to ride?" Kacy asked as she reached for the salt shaker.

He shrugged. "That's the problem. I don't know. Most things come naturally to me and I don't hesitate before doing them. Like the swimming. I just knew I could do it."

"But you don't have that feeling about riding?"

He shook his head. "It's actually just the opposite. I feel apprehensive, which doesn't make any sense since I wouldn't have applied for a job as a ranch hand if I couldn't ride...unless I'm one of those cowboy wanna-bes you mentioned."

Worried that he would see the guilt on her face she got up to get herself another cup of coffee. With her back to him, she said, "You can put your mind at rest, Austin. You've been on a horse. I've seen you ride." When she turned around again, all eyes were on her.

Austin's narrowed as he said, "I rode when I came to apply for a job?"

She answered him with a question. "Does that sound unusual? That we'd require people who wanted to work at the ranch to show us they can handle a horse?"

"No, it makes sense." He relaxed then and smiled. "Of course I can ride. I suppose it's only natural to feel apprehensive because I have no memory of it."

"I'm sure that's what it is," Dusty agreed, although Kacy could tell by the look on his face that he was not happy with her stretching the truth.

"So, do you want me to help with the cattle?" Austin asked.

Kacy shot her brother a look that implored him to say no. To her relief, he did.

"Naw, you go ahead and work for Kacy." Dusty reached for a toothpick which he used as a pointer as he said, "But I'm warning you. You better watch out for my sister. She'll work a man till he drops if you let her."

"I just gave him the day off," Kacy said in her own defense as she sat back down at the table.

"An offer which I would refuse if you'd let me," Austin told her.

"I won't let you," she said stubbornly. "I know just the place to take you. As soon as you've finished breakfast we'll go. You'll want to bring your hat though."

Again there were several cocked eyebrows.

Austin pushed his plate away and asked, "And how do I need to dress for this place?"

"You look fine the way you are. You go get your hat and meet me out by the pickup in fifteen minutes," she instructed Austin.

She thought he might protest, but he simply gave her a grin and said, "You're the boss."

As soon as he had left the kitchen, Kacy learned the meaning for all of the raised eyebrows cast in her direction. "You're getting awfully friendly with the guy, aren't you?" Dusty commented.

Kacy didn't answer. She opened the refrigerator and pulled out a jar of salad dressing and a plate of cold cuts.

"Yeah—what's going on, Kace?" Suzy wanted to know.

"Nothing's going on." She emphasized her denial by slamming the bread drawer shut.

"Yeah, right," Suzy retorted sarcastically.

"Are you sure you know what you're doing?" Mark asked.

Kacy turned and faced them all, hands on her hips. "Look. I'm twenty-six, not thirteen, and I would appreciate it if everyone would just go about their business and let me handle this situation as I see fit."

Her outburst resulted in chairs scraping against the

floor and plates being taken to the sink. One by one her family disappeared until Dusty was the only one left. He stood with one hip against the counter, arms folded across his chest, eyeing her curiously.

"So do I dare ask where you are going with him or will you snap my head off?"

"I didn't *snap* anyone's head off," she disagreed, although she knew that she had spat the words out with a bit more force than she had intended. She opened a cabinet and pulled out a basket. "We're going on a picnic."

"I thought you said you wanted to get even with this guy."

"I do."

"Going on a picnic is getting even?"

"There's no law that says I can't have fun in the process, is there?" She slathered salad dressing on several slices of bread, then piled on an assortment of lunch meats and cheeses. "It's not like he hasn't worked hard all week long. Even prisoners get recreational time. Besides, I need a break from the ranch, too."

"Where are you going for this picnic?"

She shrugged. "I'm not sure. Maybe to the Peace Garden."

"That's a hundred miles from here."

"So?"

"So what if his memory comes back when you're in the middle of nowhere? Have you thought about what he's going to do when he discovers who he really is?"

She had thought about it. A lot. Mentally she had prepared her defense, yet she didn't tell her brother that. "I'll handle it."

"Are you sure you can? He's going to be one angry man," he warned.

"You don't know that."

He made a sound of disbelief. "You're pretending he's someone else when you know his true identity! Kacy, any man would be angry about that."

She knew he had a point, but she wouldn't admit that to him. "I said I can handle it and I will."

He made a sound of frustration. "You can be so bull-headed when you want to be."

"I take that as a compliment," she said with a grin she knew would annoy him.

He only shook his head. "You know what I think? I think you ought to end this charade today. You've worked him from sunup to sundown for eight days in a row. I know that doesn't equal the sum of money he owes us, but I say you've extracted a fair amount of vengeance. Now it's time to give it up."

She dropped the knife on the counter. "Give it up? I'm not giving it up. Besides, if he's going to be angry when he learns the truth, what's the difference whether I tell him now or after he's worked awhile longer?" She licked a dab of salad dressing from her finger.

"Because this is no longer about the money."

"What do you mean?"

"Suzy's right. There's something going on between the two of you."

She couldn't prevent the blush that colored her cheeks.

"That's the real reason why you don't want to tell him the truth, isn't it? You like having the guy around and not because he's fixing stuff on your property."

She tried to make her voice sound nonchalant as she slipped the sandwiches into plastic bags. "As I said, there's no law against having fun with him, is there?"

Dusty rolled his eyes. "Having fun is one thing, fall-ing for the guy is another."

She laughed nervously. "I'm not falling for anyone."

"You better not be. He's a suit, not a cowboy, and in case you've forgotten, the guy's a jerk. You said so yourself."

"That was the CEO Austin. This Austin's a cowboy with amnesia and he's been nothing but nice this week."

He groaned in frustration. "Of course he's been nice. He has to be. He's at our mercy. Without us, there's no roof over his head, no food to eat."

"That isn't why," she argued.

"What? You think some bump on the head made him into a better person?" he asked in disbelief. "Have you forgotten that this is the guy who took great pleasure in making your life miserable not so long ago?"

She had forgotten. And she didn't want to be reminded right now. "I know what I'm doing," she said with more confidence than she was feeling.

"I doubt that."

"I do." She put the sandwiches into the picnic basket, along with a bunch of grapes, some crackers, cheese and a couple of wine coolers.

It was the last item that really raised Dusty's thick eyebrows. "Wine coolers?"

Kacy ignored him, snapping the lid shut. "We'll be back later."

"Don't forget it's Sunday. The ranch hands may not have to work, but we do. We have a group of pharmaceutical people coming in time for dinner."

"I'll be here," she assured him, then hurried out to the pickup.

"YOU MAKE A pretty good tour guide." Austin was getting used to the picture of Kacy Judd behind the wheel of the truck. He wished she didn't have her hair tucked up under her hat, however. With the windows down, he could only imagine how those red tresses would look blowing in the wind.

"Am I boring you?" she asked, giving him a side-ways glance. It had its usual effect on him. Parts of his anatomy jumped to attention and he quickly looked away.

"No. It's not boring at all," he assured her, turning his attention to the seemingly endless vista of prairie outside his window. "It's interesting."

She cocked her head, her eyes squinting. "Yes, but is it necessary? Maybe you know just as much about this area as I do."

"If I do, I don't remember it," he answered candidly.

"Look. We're getting close enough so that you can see the Turtle Mountains."

For the past hour they had seen nothing but flat farm-land dotted with an occasional grain elevator or oil well. Now, wooded hills could be seen in the distance, rising out of the treeless plain. As they got closer he could see the steeply rolling uplands were covered with aspen and birch.

"Those are mountains? They seem more like high-lands to me."

"I suppose people who live in the Rockies would call them hills, but to us they're mountains," she told him as she drove into the grassy footlands.

Austin expected her to pull into a roadside picnic area or stop at one of the sandy white beaches on any of the lakes they passed. She didn't. She kept driving until she came to a sign that indicated they were approaching the International Peace Garden.

"Is this where we're going to have our picnic?" he

asked as she followed the signs directing her to the parking area.

"Umm-hmm. It's one of my favorite spots…and not just because it's full of beautiful flowers. You'll see what I mean." She hopped out of the truck, leaving the picnic basket inside. "We'll come back for the food after we've looked at the gardens."

She led him along a walkway that wound through the woods, past several fountains, and a crystal pool until they came to a plaza with two tall towering cement monuments that Austin thought resembled giant H's.

"That's the Peace Tower." She pointed to a stone cairn that read, We Two Nations Dedicate This Garden And Pledge That As Long As Men Shall Live We Will Not Take Up Arms Against One Another.

"We're at the Canadian border then?"

She nodded. "This is the midpoint of the longest peaceful border in the world." She pointed in the opposite direction. "Over there is a fountain and a moat which marks the exact spot. Want to go look?"

He nodded and she led him past beautifully manicured lawns and colorful flower gardens. Again she acted as a tour guide. Austin thought to himself that even if he had been here before and knew most of what she was saying, he wouldn't have told her. He loved listening to her talk and watching her face change expressively.

After they had seen the flower gardens, they returned to the truck to get the picnic basket and a plaid blanket. Then she led him down a paved trail that led to a pristine lake. Not far from the crystal clear water she spread the blanket on the velvety lawn, kicked off her boots, motioning for him to sit down beside her.

"We have a feast fit for a king and queen," she announced as she pulled their lunch out of the basket and set it on the blanket.

He reached for a bottle of wine cooler and studied the label. "Very Berry?"

"I also brought soda if you'd rather have that," she told him.

"No, this is good." He twisted off the cap and took a swallow. "Thanks for bringing me here. This is a nice place for a picnic."

"I love it here. It's so peaceful—just as its name says." She removed her hat, allowing her cinnamon curls to spring free. Austin had to fight the urge to tame their waywardness with his fingers. He, too, removed his hat, setting it next to hers on the corner of the blanket.

She offered him a sandwich. "Roast beef or turkey?"

He chose the roast beef. While they ate they talked mostly about the ranch, but Austin wasn't interested in her family or the livestock or the retreat center. He wanted to know more about her.

When she mentioned that several of her horses had been on the rodeo circuit, he said, "Mark told me that you're a top-notch barrel racer."

"I have a few trophies on the shelf," she said modestly.

"How many is a few?"

She shrugged sheepishly. "Maybe twenty or thirty."

"That's a few?"

"I started barrel racing when I was just a kid."

"He said that you've tried bull riding, too."

She dabbed at her mouth with a napkin. "Talkative man, my brother Mark."

"Did you stay on?"

"What do you think?"

He grinned. "I guess that's a silly question isn't it. Of course you did."

"I'm not as skinny as I look. Besides, I've been breaking horses since I was a teenager."

"Can't you get hurt doing that?"

She laughed. "You can get hurt getting out of bed if you're not careful. So what else did my big brother tell you about me?"

"That you lived in New York for a while and hated every minute of it."

"Not every minute," she corrected. "There were a few of them I liked."

"I'm surprised you left the ranch. It's such a big part of your life," he observed.

"It *is* my life."

"Then why leave?"

She paused to finish chewing before she answered. "I thought I should see more of the world besides this little corner of it. So I went, worked for a while, got it out of my system, then came home."

"Where did you work?"

"At an art gallery."

"You like art?"

"Yes. That surprises you?"

He studied her for a moment before saying, "No. Should it?"

"Not many people expect a cowgirl would have a degree in art history," she answered. "The truth is I went to a small liberal arts college just southeast of here."

"That would explain why the lodge corridors are lined with art."

"I love art almost as much as I love horses. That's

why I made sure I went to a college that had a saddle club,'' she told him, smiling wistfully at the thought.

"So you went to New York after you graduated?"

"The ink was barely dry on my diploma when I packed my bags and headed for the Big Apple." She washed down a bite of sandwich with a sip of wine. "Boy, what a case of culture shock that was. Do you know there are more people in one borough of New York City than there are in the whole state of North Dakota?"

She didn't wait for him to answer, but continued on, "I mean, after living on the ranch it would have been hard enough moving to a city the size of Fargo, but New York..." she trailed off, shaking her head.

"Was it hard?"

"Umm-hmm. Especially the first few months. I was homesick. That was something I never expected because I had spent four years away at college. But being away at college and living in a city like New York are not exactly the same thing."

"I'm surprised you stayed three years."

"I wanted to make sure I gave it a fair chance. Plus, I wanted to show my dad that he hadn't wasted his money on my education."

"Money on education is never wasted."

She glanced at him sideways. "No, you're right. It isn't."

"Was your father disappointed when you decided you'd rather be on the ranch than selling artwork?"

"Not really. You see while I was gone my brothers had convinced him that they had the perfect solution to the Triple J's financial problems."

"Turning it into a dude ranch?"

"More of a conference center with a western setting.

Dad figured if he was going to hire someone to give riding lessons, it might as well be me.''

"Is that why you came home? To help out at the ranch?"

"Partly." She paused to take a sip of the wine cooler. "I realized working in an art gallery was not what I wanted to do with my life." She sighed and looked out across the lake. "When I look at all this, I often wonder how I lasted as long as I did."

"Is that regret I hear in your voice?"

"Not really. It was a good experience for me and it made me realize what I really want in life."

"And that is?"

"To work with horses, to live in a place where the air is clean, the water fresh, where towns are small and people know each other. I want to be able to look out my window and see nothing but open space."

"Is there room for a man in that picture?"

"Maybe...if I can find one who fits in."

"No one in New York did?"

She chuckled. "No. None even came close. I don't need a walking stock market report and the only futures I care about are the ones that belong to my horses."

"So you've never been married?"

Again she chuckled. "No."

"Engaged?"

"No."

"Seriously involved with anyone?"

She hesitated and he quickly added, "I knew there has to have been somebody. The men of New York would have had to have been blind not to notice you."

"Believe me. When you have hair the color of mine, you get noticed."

"And rightly so."

She glanced sideways at him again and his heart fluttered. "Are you flirting with me, Austin?"

"I don't think I remember what flirting is," he teased, needing to put the conversation on a lighter tone or risk sliding over and planting kisses up and down her pretty little neck.

"Oh, I think you do," she teased right back. She reached over to snatch his empty paper plate from him and toss it into the picnic hamper. As she bent, her hair fell across her cheek.

Austin couldn't resist the urge to reach over and push it back from her face. "Do you have any idea how you make me feel?"

She stopped clearing away the remains of the picnic lunch and looked at him. "How?" It was barely above a whisper, her lips parting ever so slightly as she waited for his answer.

He leaned over and placed a soft kiss on her mouth. "Like I'm somebody."

"You are somebody, Austin."

"I am when I am with you." He planted another butterfly kiss on her mouth. "Thank you."

She eased away from him, fidgeting nervously with the latch on the picnic basket, her eyes downcast.

He grabbed her by the shoulders so that she was staring up at him. "I'm not flirting with you, Kacy. It's true. For the past week I've been struggling with who I am, trying to unravel the mystery of my past. I have no idea what kind of man I was or whether or not I'd even like that man. All I know is that when I'm with you, I like who I am."

The air was suddenly charged with sexual tension as silence stretched between them. He studied her face, amazed by how easily he had committed it to his mem-

ory and how often it came to mind while he was working
at her house. It was not the face he expected to find on
someone who spent long days in the sun. Except for the
scant dusting of freckles across her cheekbones, her skin
was fair. He liked the fact that she wore very little
makeup. Her mouth, her nose and her cheekbones all
had a delicacy which gave her a feminine look. But it
was her green eyes he found most interesting. They always appeared to be focused on the horizon, yet she
didn't miss a single move he made.

It was a face he would never get tired of looking at.
One he wanted to see lying on the pillow next to his at
night. He began to plant kisses on her neck, loving the
feel of her warm flesh beneath his lips.

She relaxed against him, tilting her head as he pushed
aside the springing red curls to nuzzle the creamy
smooth skin. His hands slid to her waist where they
rested briefly, before slowly making a journey up her rib
cage. Her breath caught in her throat as his thumbs
moved to just below her breasts.

"I think you like who *I* am, too," he whispered as he
continued to place kisses on every smooth surface he
could find. Her cheeks, her chin, her neck, her ears, until
finally her arms wrapped themselves around his neck.

With an intensity that left little doubt about her feelings for him, she kissed him long and hard, her tongue
working its way into his mouth to ignite a thousand fires
inside him. Together they fell to the blanket, mouths
locked, legs tangled, hands exploring. A low groan came
from his throat as she rubbed against him hungrily, her
body as pliant and as willing as his.

When the wild hungry kisses ended, he was leaning
over her. Her shirt was unbuttoned, her breasts heaving,
threatening to fall out of the flimsy pieces of satin trying

to confine them. He kissed the bulging flesh, fighting the temptation to push aside the fabric and take all of her into his mouth. It didn't help that she had unbuttoned his shirt and slid her fingers inside, caressing him in a way that made him want to forget they were in a public park.

"This isn't the best place for this, is it?" he asked in between kisses.

As if to prove his point, a duck quacked nearby. She chuckled. "No, but sometimes it can be fun to live a little dangerously." There was a teasing light in her eyes, one that he knew masked desire.

He planted two more kisses, one on each of her breasts, then with a sigh, buttoned her shirt. Before he could roll away, she pulled his mouth to hers and kissed him one last time, taking him by surprise.

As soon as she ended the kiss, she became almost aloof. She finished buttoning her shirt, making sure it was tucked inside her jeans before getting to her feet. Without a word she packed away the picnic things and folded the blanket.

Not once on the ride home did she say anything about what had happened between them. Austin was beginning to think that either she wanted to forget that it had happened or else she regretted encouraging him.

But then, when she dropped him off at the bunkhouse she asked, "How about if we do something dangerous at my place tomorrow night?"

Austin tipped his hat and said, "I'll be there."

KACY IGNORED THE looks she got from her family that evening. While the new group at the lodge went through the orientation dinner, she sat quietly, thinking about her day with Austin. It had been perfect—or as perfect as it could be considering the circumstances.

Her whole body warmed at the memory of how good it had felt to be in his arms. She still couldn't believe that he had been the one to stop their lovemaking when he did. She had been so wild with desire for him she had totally forgotten that they were indeed in a very public place. Her face flamed at the thought. She could just imagine what her brothers and Suzy would say if they knew what had really happened that afternoon.

Although she went through the motions at dinner and during the meeting afterward, her mind was not on team building. It was on Austin and what they were going to do tomorrow night. She would cook a romantic dinner for two, put some slow dance music on the stereo and…

"Kacy, phone call."

Her musings were interrupted by her sister.

"Who is it?"

Suzy shrugged. "I don't know. Some woman. She wouldn't give me her name. Just insisted that she talk to you."

Kacy left the conference room and went to the front desk where one line on the phone console blinked. She pushed down the button and picked up the receiver.

"This is Kacy Judd. How may I help you?"

"This is Daphne Delattre. Austin Bennett's fiancée."

Kacy's heart started to thud in her throat.

"I'm hoping you can help me," the smooth voice said.

"And how would I be able to do that?" Kacy asked cautiously.

"I'm afraid Austin's missing."

"Missing?" By now Kacy felt as if a herd of horses were stampeding in her chest.

"He told his secretary that he was taking a vacation, but he isn't with relatives in Montana, which is where everyone thought he would be."

"I don't understand. What does that have to do with me, Ms. Delattre?" she said, amazed by how calm her voice sounded.

"I'm wondering if maybe he wasn't so impressed by the program you offer that he decided to return and learn more about it so he could be more effective with his own employees."

Kacy had to stifle the urge to laugh out loud. Daphne Delattre did not know Austin Bennett very well if she thought that. "Mr. Bennett did not return to the ranch to learn anything, Ms. Delattre. To be perfectly honest, he hated it while he was here."

"Then where is he?"

"If his secretary says he's on vacation then he must be on vacation"

Her answer did not please the other woman. "Austin doesn't take vacations! Something is wrong with this picture. He wouldn't just take off like that—not when he knew we were supposed to be at the Carlton Benefit this weekend."

Kacy had a sick feeling in the pit of her stomach and not because she was lying to Daphne Delattre. What she realized now was that Austin had another life—a life that involved another woman and another world very different from hers.

"I'm sorry, Ms. Delattre. I can't help you."

Daphne finally rung off but not before leaving all sorts of instructions as to what she wanted Kacy to do should Austin show up at the ranch. By the time the phone call was over, Kacy was shaking.

"What's wrong?" Suzy asked when she met her in the hallway.

"Nothing. I'm fine," Kacy answered, but the truth was she not fine at all. She was caught in the middle of a very big lie. And that lie involved a man whom she wanted more than anything in the world to convince she was a decent, honest person.

Talk about living dangerously.

Chapter Eleven

"When I'm with you, I feel like I'm somebody."

Austin's words echoed in Kacy's mind as she watched him climb out of her orange pickup wearing the fanciest white shirt she had ever seen. A dancin' shirt is what Suzy would have called it. Together with the bolo tie he wore around his neck, it made him look more like a cowboy on a date.

He was her date. A thought which made her all tingly. She had loaned him the truck so that he could go back and get cleaned up after he had finished working at her place. But he wasn't just cleaned up. He was looking great and in his hands he carried a bouquet of flowers.

"I must say, Mr. Beaumont, that you clean up quite nicely for a cowboy. New threads?" she said as he approached the verandah.

"The crook who robbed me didn't get every last cent I own," he confessed. "The first night I was here I discovered he missed a pocket where I had stuck a hundred-dollar bill. I was waiting for a special occasion to use it."

The fact that he thought tonight special made Kacy's heart swell.

"These are for you. I had Suzy pick them up in town since I didn't have any way of getting there."

She accepted the flowers and sniffed them appreciatively. "Thank you. They're lovely, but you shouldn't have spent your last dollar on me."

"I only wish I had some money. Then I'd be able to court you properly," he said with a tenderness that made Kacy's heart ache.

She swallowed back a tear and said, "Come on inside and I'll put these in some water."

He followed her into the house, looking about curiously. Kacy realized that it was the first time she had asked him inside. For a week they'd been eating supper out on the verandah.

She didn't want to call attention to the fact, yet she needed to say something. So she said, "I don't spend much time in here in the summer. It just seems like a waste of time to be inside when it's so beautiful outside," she told him, although she knew that it wasn't the true reason why she had kept him on the porch. She hadn't wanted him in her space, because with every little bit she gave him, he became more important to her. And that was a scary thought.

Only now, seeing him standing in her living room with his hat in his hands, she liked the way he looked. It was as if he was supposed to be there. And she knew that he already had a place in her heart whether she wanted him to be there or not.

"Go ahead and look around while I put these in some water," she told him, then disappeared into the kitchen. When she returned, he was studying a rolltop desk that she had inherited from one of her great-uncles.

"This is in beautiful condition," he said pulling open a tiny drawer.

"Isn't it though? It belonged to my grandmother's brother who was a banker. I remember going over to visit him as a child and always being afraid to touch anything in his home for fear of putting a fingerprint on it."

"This is solid oak. They don't make them like this anymore. So many products are veneer finished." He continued to appraise the desk, giving Kacy a moment of anxiety. Was this where one of the bits of memory would occur? She held her breath, waiting for what was to come.

Nothing did. When he finally noticed the wine in her hands, he straightened and smiled.

"I brought you something to drink." She handed him a glass.

He took a sip, then looked around the room. Just when she thought the easy camaraderie that had been with them at the Peace Garden yesterday would transfer into this evening, an awkward tension settled between them. Kacy wasn't sure why. She worried that it was because he might be regaining those bits and pieces of his memory as her grandfather had predicted. Or maybe it was the fact that this was more of a date.

Whatever the reason, Kacy wasn't sure how to put things back on the right track. Dinner went well. They cooked the steaks outside, but rather than eat at the picnic table, she set her small round wooden table in the kitchen with a white linen cloth and silver. Instead of the neon ceiling light, candles lit the room, setting the atmosphere for an intimate dinner for two. The wine helped Kacy to relax a bit, but she felt like a schoolgirl waiting for her date to make that first move and give her a kiss. He appeared to be just as uneasy as she was.

When they had finished eating, Kacy automatically

began cleaning up. He came up behind her while she was standing at the sink rinsing off the plates and said, "I'd say anytime the Triple J needs a new cook they don't have to look very far."

She turned so that their faces were only inches apart. "I take it you liked dinner?"

"Umm-hmm. Food was good, company was..." His eyes roved over her face and Kacy felt her breath catch in her throat. "...the company was exactly what this cowboy needed after a hard day."

"Boss work you too hard?" she teased.

"Uh-uh. The hard part was waiting for this evening to come. I like being with you, Kacy."

"I like being with you, too, Austin." She wiped her hands on the towel, needing to look away from those penetrating blue eyes.

Another awkward silence threatened to totally ruin the evening. Then, unable to stand the tension, she decided to be the one to break the ice. She grabbed him and kissed him long and hard on the mouth. Judging by his reaction, it was exactly what he had been wanting as well.

"I figured if I didn't do that pretty soon we were going to be walking on eggshells all night and we wouldn't get to the living dangerously part."

He grinned, his eyes brimming with desire.

She fingered one of the pearly snaps on his shirt. "You do want to live dangerously, don't you?"

"I wouldn't be here if I didn't," he answered.

An idea had been simmering at the back of her mind all day long. Only until he had arrived, she wasn't sure that she was going to be able to go through with it. Now she knew that this was her opportunity to be bold and daring.

"Great. Then wait here and I'll be right back." She went in search of a couple of large white towels. When she returned with them to the kitchen, Austin looked puzzled.

She didn't explain, but pulled him by the hand and led him out the back door. "Come with me."

It was a perfect summer evening, the air still warm, the wind calm. The sun sat like a golden egg on the nest of trees lining the horizon, giving a gilded glow to the sky. Kacy felt as if they could be a couple of wood sprites scrambling through the twilight.

"Where are we going?" he asked as she dragged him down the back steps and through the grass.

"For a swim."

He stopped her with a tug on her hands. "But I didn't bring my trunks."

She looked him right in the eye and she said with an impish grin, "That's the dangerous part."

A grin spread slowly across his face, lighting up his eyes. "You want to go naked?"

"It's called skinny-dipping, in case you've forgotten."

"I know what it's called. I'm just not sure I've ever done it with a date."

"Good. Cuz I haven't, either."

"I don't believe you."

She continued to pull him by the hand until they were at the water's edge. "All right. So I might have done it once when I was a little kid."

"What do you classify as little kid? Sixteen?"

She ignored his questions and shoved him toward a big fat oak tree. "You undress here and I'll go behind those bushes over there."

She started to walk away, but he called out to her, "Wait! Are you taking off *all* your clothes?"

She gave him a seductive smile. "Ever heard of anyone skinny-dipping in their underwear?"

He grinned back. "Just checking."

Her hands trembled as she undid the buttons on her blouse. She knew she would have never suggested skinny-dipping with any other man, but with Austin, she felt like being bold. Now that she had given her heart to him, there seemed to be no point in wasting any time they had together. If their relationship was to be short, she wanted it to be sweet.

When she had removed everything except her bra and bikini briefs, she peeked around the brambling bushes. Austin stood at the water's edge, the white towel draped around his waist.

"You're not getting cold feet, are you?" he asked when he saw her sneak a peek.

She popped back behind the bushes guiltily. "Not me," she called out, shedding her undergarments.

"Good. I like the Kacy who's not afraid to try anything."

It was all the encouragement she needed. "Okay, I'm ready! On the count of three, in the water! One! Two! Three..." she shouted, then went streaking for the river. Whether or not he watched, she didn't know. She was in too big a hurry to get her naked body submerged.

When she surfaced, he was beside her, shaking the water from his head. "Well? What do you think?" she asked.

"It feels good," he answered. "I think the water's warmer than the air."

"That's why I like swimming at this time of day." She leaned back and floated on her back, staring up at the sky. "Don't you just love the way the setting sun makes everything look almost mystical? It's like someone's put a huge amber filter on the camera and we're captured in this moment of time."

"I've been feeling that way for a while...actually, ever since I met you," he said, moving closer to her. "I've lost a big part of time, but I've found something magical here in the past ten days."

He reached for her, his hands finding her waist. The river was just deep enough that she needed to tread to keep her chin above water, but he was tall enough to stand. "Float against me," he murmured, urging her to come closer. "I won't let you go under. Just wrap your legs around my waist." The look in his eyes sent a thrill of anticipation through her.

Kacy knew what would happen if she did as he suggested. Although the water was dark and he wouldn't be able to see her body parts, he certainly would be able to feel them. And she would be able to feel his. Excitement gushed through her.

She told herself that she should swim away. With a playful slap against the water she could make their swim a frolic instead of a sensory exploration. She could. If she wanted to.

She didn't want to. She wanted to be in his arms, feeling the strength of his hard, wet body. She wanted to know what it was like to press her naked flesh up against his. So like a mermaid she snaked her slender legs around his waist and reached for his broad shoulders.

He made certain she was exactly where he wanted her, using his hands to find the curve of her buttocks and pull her even closer. When she was locked against him, his eyes flared with a satisfaction that sent heat rushing through her.

"I like the way this feels," he said, his gaze holding hers.

She deliberately misunderstood him. "It's good to feel the water gently moving against us, isn't it?"

"That's not what I was talking about," he answered, his voice dropping to a husky purr that made Kacy feel as if he had control over every sensitive spot on her.

With her legs locked at his back and her hands clinging to his shoulders, he bobbed up and down in the water, causing tiny waves to caress her shoulders. He didn't need to hold on to her which meant he could use his hands for other things.

And he did. Like pushing her wet hair away from her neck so he could plant kisses in the most sensitive places. Under her chin. Behind her ear. On her shoulder.

"It's much more fun swimming with you than swimming alone," he murmured close to her ear.

"I have to admit, Austin. You're teaching me some new things about skinny-dipping," she said huskily as his roving hands found her breasts. Hearing the rush of air she inhaled, he smiled a delightfully wicked smile that told her he knew exactly what his fingers were doing to her.

Then he captured her mouth with his, in a kiss that was not only hot, but demanding. Kacy opened her lips, reveling in the intimate exploration his tongue made. Desire carried them away, as if it were a current in the river, dragging them down, deeper and deeper into a passionate exploration of their senses.

Kacy found herself floating on a sea of longing. Every kiss left her craving another, wanting to feel the heat of his fingers on her wet flesh. Instinctively her body rubbed against his, and as it did she felt the proof of his desire for her. Over and over, hot pleasure rippled through her, at the thought of how close she was to having him inside her.

When he pulled his mouth away from hers, his eyes were as dark as the night time river. "I want to make love to you, Kacy, but I'm a little rusty at this."

She unwrapped her legs from around his waist, allowing them to fall. She was able to capture his manhood between her legs, sliding down on it until he was poised at the entrance to her womanhood. "It doesn't feel like it's rusty," she told him, holding him tightly to her.

She could feel him tremble as she used the buoyancy of the water to tease him, carefully moving up and down on him. Finally, when she herself could no long resist, she lowered herself on his shaft. She sighed as it slid inside smoothly. "No, this definitely isn't rusty. I do believe it's going to work just fine."

A groan of ecstasy scraped the back of his throat as he cupped her buttocks and pushed himself deeper inside her. Any control Kacy had was gone as with powerful thrusts he swept away any doubt that he had forgotten what it meant to make love. She clung to him, matching his movements with a frantic rhythm of her own until neither one could hold back the waves of pleasure that had them clinging to each other in a sea of ecstasy.

When the climax came, it was his strength that kept them from sinking under the water. Out of breath and trembling, Kacy gasped as he gently eased away from her. She suddenly felt empty and had to struggle to stay afloat.

"Come on. You're cold. I'll help you swim to shore," he told her, turning her onto her back so he could tow her to shore.

"I'm not cold," she told him, wanting him to understand that the trembling had nothing to do with the water.

"You're trembling."

"Well, yeah. Look what just happened."

He didn't say that it had been an earth-shattering experience for him, too. He simply swam toward the shore, pulling her along with him. As their feet touched ground, Austin grabbed her by the waist and hoisted her to her feet. She felt like a rag doll, ready to flop over in any direction. He noticed her unsteadiness and swept her up into his arms. He carried her up the embankment and didn't put her down until he had spotted her clothes. He grabbed one of the fluffy white towels, then draped it around her shivering form.

When he slapped at his skin with the palm of his hand, she said, "Mosquitoes."

He swatted madly. "They're everywhere!"

"Yup." She slipped her feet into her boots, got partially dressed then headed for the house, waving at him as she zipped on by. "We'd better hurry or we'll have more bites than we can scratch."

She ran all the way back to the house, not waiting to see if he was following. Once inside, she turned around and saw that he had wasted no time, either. She giggled at the sight of Austin standing in her kitchen wearing nothing but his boots, his boxers and the fancy dancing shirt. Only he wasn't exactly wearing the shirt. It only had a couple of snaps fastened and they were uneven, making it sit cockeyed on his muscular torso. In one arm were his scrunched-up jeans, and dangling from one of his fingers was her pink satin bra. Kacy figured she must have dropped it in her haste to get home.

"I can see you haven't had much experience getting

dressed in a hurry, cowboy,'' she said, running her eyes up and down his figure.

''I'd like to see you pull on a pair of jeans over wet skin.'' He tossed the jeans on the chair, then stepped closer to her. He held the pink satin bra up for her inspection. ''It's a pretty little thing but it sure doesn't look big enough to be yours.''

Kacy felt her skin grow warm. She took the bra from his fingertips and said, ''I guess there's no point in being modest now, is there?'' She returned his wicked grin with one of her own.

''Guess not,'' he agreed unabashedly. ''I may not have a memory, but I'm certain I've never done that kind of skinny-dipping before.''

''Well, I'll tell you what. I do have a memory and I know I've never done that before.''

He moved closer to her and slipped his hands around her waist. ''Never?''

She felt her heart pump faster and her breath caught in her throat at the memory of their lovemaking. ''Not like *that*.''

''Is that good?''

''Umm-hmm.'' She began to undo the uneven snaps on his shirt. ''It means that tonight was special and that is definitely good.''

''I'm glad to hear that. From the look on your face when I towed you back to shore I was worried that you were either hurt or feeling regret.''

''That was disappointment,'' she said, then added quickly, ''Because I wasn't ready for it to be over. You didn't hurt me, and I definitely don't feel any regret.'' Instead of snapping the shirt closed again, she slid her fingers inside the polished cotton, loving the feel of his warm flesh beneath her palms as she placed her hands on his chest.

He captured her hands and raised them to his lips. "I wouldn't blame you if you weren't feeling a little apprehensive. Things have happened so fast between us and you know so little about me. For all you know I could have baggage in my past. I could have commitments, responsibilities...."

"What makes you think I don't?"

"Because you're the not the kind of woman to lead a man on."

"And you can tell that by spending what—ten days—here?"

He moved a wet strand of hair from her cheek to the mass of curls plastered to her head. "Yeah. I knew it the minute I saw you at Bill Cox's place. Call it intuition or a gut feeling or whatever, but I believe that even with amnesia I'm a pretty good judge of character. I doubt there's a dishonest bone in your body."

Guilt had her swallowing with difficulty. "Maybe one or two little bitty ones might be a teensy bit crooked," she said with a nervous giggle, turning her head to avoid his intense gaze.

He put a finger under her chin and turned her face back to his. "I'm serious, Kacy. What happened out there in the river...well, it was good. So good that it made me forget I'm a man without a past."

"I don't care about your past, Austin," she told him, putting her hands once more on his chest.

"Maybe you should."

"No. All that matters is what's happening to us now. Maybe it is risky, but you ought to know, I'm not a woman who plays it safe." To emphasize her point she slowly slid her hands down his stomach until they rested on the waistband of his boxers. "I'm not going to let you play it safe, either."

"That sounds like a threat," he said, his breath a bit uneven as she eased the tips of her fingers inside the elastic.

"Uh-uh. Think of it as a promise." The look in his eyes sent a shiver of delightful anticipation through her. "And I'm going to warn you. I always keep my promises." She pulled her fingers free, allowing the waistband to snap back.

"You can trust me, Kacy. I'll never hurt you. And that's a promise."

"I do trust you." It was an honest declaration. Kacy knew that he would never deliberately hurt her…at least the Austin he was now wouldn't.

"Good." He kissed her softly on the lips.

"Now that that's settled. I have to ask you two questions."

He opened his palms. "Ask away."

"Do you want a passion fruit wine cooler?"

"Sounds like the perfect way to end the evening." He watched her open the refrigerator and pull out two bottles. "What's the second question?"

"Are you going to put those jeans on tonight or do you want to wait until the morning?"

IT WASN'T AN alarm that woke Kacy but the smell of coffee. Opening her eyes she saw a rose on her pillow. She smiled. Austin was in her kitchen. As she raised her head her temples throbbed.

She fell back against the pillow, covering her eyes with her forearm, blaming her headache and Austin's presence on the wine coolers. If she hadn't been drink-

ng, she wouldn't be struggling to lift her head and Aus-
in wouldn't have spent the night.

She chastised herself mentally. Who was she fooling?
She had asked him to stay *before* she had opened the
passion fruit wine coolers.

As memories of last night flooded her mind, her body
ingled. She had thought that what had happened in the
iver had been about as good as it gets. Then they had
put on a k.d. lang CD, slow danced naked in her living
oom, and what had followed made their earlier lovemaking seem like foreplay. For a guy who had no rec-
ollection of ever making love to a woman, he had all
the right moves.

Basic instinct. That's what he had called it. But Kacy
knew it was more than that. It was as if his body had
been made to fit hers. And it wasn't just the physical
aspect of their lovemaking. Their minds had come together in the same type of union. Kacy knew that no
matter what happened in the future, she would always
have the memory of last night.

The thought of the future had her pushing herself to
get up. What she had with Austin was so good, yet it
was so fragile. Any day his memory could return and
then... She pulled on a cotton wrap and forced those
thoughts from her mind. She didn't want to think about
the future. She only wanted to enjoy today.

She found Austin in the kitchen at the stove. He was
shirtless, his only clothes his jeans slung low on his hips.
At the sound of her entrance, he turned and grinned. A
wide, wonderful grin that made Kacy wish they never
had to leave her house again.

"I was going to bring you breakfast in bed, but I'm
afraid I must not know how to cook. These eggs look
awful."

Kacy glanced at the glob of yellow and white with burnt edges and smiled affectionately. "I'm not an egg person anyway."

He turned off the stove and pulled her into his arms. His mouth covered hers in a long, sensuous exploration that reminded Kacy of the power those lips had over her.

"Good morning," he said against her lips.

She snuggled against his chest, loving the feeling of being wrapped in his arms. "Morning came much too quickly for me," she confessed.

He held her close, kissing the top of her head. "We didn't get much sleep."

She grinned against his warm flesh. "Nope." With a sigh, she finally pushed him away. "I need to get ready for work."

He nodded in understanding. "I need to change my clothes."

Suddenly reality stared Kacy in the face. "You want to go back to the ranch."

He grinned. "I don't want to work in my courting clothes."

The polished cotton white shirt still lay across a kitchen chair. "No. That shirt is made for dancing. Did you know that?"

"We did dance last night," he reminded her.

She couldn't prevent the grin or the blush that spread across her face. "That's such a fancy shirt and being you spent your last dollar on it, I think I ought to take you someplace where you can show it off. Like the Buckle Bar. They've got a great country western band there every Tuesday night."

"Then I definitely don't want to get it dirty today."

Suddenly he closed his eyes and ran his fingers across his brow.

"You have a headache, too?" she asked.

He didn't answer immediately, but stood quietly for several moments. When he did open his eyes, they had a strange, faraway look in them.

"No. My head is fine. I just had this picture in my mind."

Kacy's heart moved up into her throat. "What kind of picture?"

"I was on a boat and there were lots of people drinking...they were all dressed up."

"Maybe it's one of those pieces my grandfather talked about."

He rubbed his forehead again. "Why would I have been on a boat?"

She shrugged uneasily. "Maybe you took a cruise or something."

"Maybe." He didn't appear to be convinced.

"Are you okay?" she asked, placing a hand on his arm.

He smiled then, the warm wonderful smile she was getting so used to seeing on his face. "I'm fine. It was just a bit unsettling. It was such a clear picture but it was so brief. I expected more..." he trailed off.

Wanting to change the subject, Kacy said, "I need to get to work, but first I want to show you something."

She motioned for him to follow her, then led him out of the kitchen and up the staircase leading to the second floor.

"This is where I like to be most of the time."

Windows on every side of the house provided the natural light necessary for Kacy to use the second floor loft as a studio. Very few people had seen the room which housed not only her art, but a small library as well.

"You're a portrait artist?"

She nodded. "I can see that surprises you."

"You said art history, not studio arts. Did you do the portraits in the lodge?"

"Some of them. I did the pastels of my great-grandfather, my grandfather and my father. They are the Triple J."

He studied her latest pastel—a full-length portrait of her cousin Linda in her wedding gown. "This is beautiful."

The sincerity in his voice sent a shiver down her spine. "Thank you."

"You could be famous." Then rolling his eyes in self-recrimination he added, "Are you famous and I just don't recognize your name because of my memory loss?"

She chuckled. "No, I'm not famous. Nor do I plan to be."

He looked around the room with an interested eye. "This is quite a studio."

"Well, it's actually more than a studio. It's where I come when I want to be by myself. Do a little daydreaming. When I designed the house, my brothers and my dad thought I should divide it into two spaces—one for working, the other for relaxing."

"But you told them working on your art is relaxing."

"How did you guess?"

He shrugged. "I just knew, that's all." He glanced at the stereo system. "You wanted to be able to listen to music while you work."

"Yes, and take a nap if I felt like it," she said, her eyes on the pillow back sofa. "I have a small refrigerator, a hot plate, a bathroom and the skylights let the sun in during the day and the stars at night...it's perfect."

"And books." He walked over to the built-in book-cases, glancing at some of the titles.

He appeared to be fascinated by her loft, taking time to examine every work of art she had, including wire sculptures she had created while in college. Kacy didn't say a word, but watched as he made a survey of the room.

"I don't let many people up here," she finally said.

"No. I can understand why not. Being in this room is like getting a glimpse into your soul."

It was exactly how she felt. When he frowned she had to ask, "Do you like what you see?"

He pulled her into his arms and hugged her close. "Of course I do. It's just that seeing all of this reminds me that you know who you are. There are no uncertainties, no unknowns in your past."

"I told you, Austin. I don't care about your past."

"I care." He lifted her chin to study her face. "What's happening between us...it's incredible."

"But?" she prodded. "I can see by the look in your eyes there's a but coming here."

When he didn't answer she pushed herself out of his arms, her back stiffening as she said, "Look, Austin, if you're trying to tell me that last night was a mistake, just say it."

In a flash he had his arms around her and his mouth locked with hers. He kissed her long and hard, leaving no doubt in her mind that he had no regrets about last night. When he raised his head, his eyes were dark.

"All I'm saying is that you're a complete picture. I'm not. And I want to be. For you." This time his kiss was gentle.

Kacy knew that what was happening between them demanded that she be honest with him. If she wanted their relationship to have any chance of succeeding, she needed to tell him the truth about why he was at the ranch.

And she would. Soon. She just wanted a few more days to be Kacy Judd and Austin Beaumont. And she wanted more nights.

"Look. We can't change the past—even if we were to know about it. But we can make right now count. And I want it to count, Austin."

"Me, too." Again, he kissed her. "I don't want to see anything mess up what we've got going for us."

"Nothing will," she assured him, but her heart feared that wasn't true.

She wanted to believe that last night meant there was a chance that he would understand why she had allowed him to believe he was a cowboy when in fact he was a Chicago businessman. That's why she decided that she would tell him the truth herself.

At the end of the week. She needed time. To get up her courage. To live a fantasy for just a few more days.

BY THE END OF the week, Kacy knew that the inevitable had to happen. Austin had had several more flashes of memory, none long enough, however to play any significant part in his discovery of his true identity. Kacy knew she was living on borrowed time. That's why she made the most of the week.

Every minute they weren't working they spent together. She taught him to do the two-step at the Buckle Bar, she took him riding along one of her favorite trails, and she showed him how to make applesauce cookies for her horses. They were seldom apart, except for the time when she needed to take care of her duties at the ranch.

It was a magical week for Kacy. By Saturday she knew that she had fallen head over heels in love with Austin. And she knew that if she wanted a chance for their relationship to work, she needed to tell him the truth.

In honor of her grandfather's birthday, the Judd ranch was to be the site of a barbecue that evening. Kacy knew that she wasn't the only one uncomfortable with the pretense. The longer Austin remained at the ranch, the more uneasy her family members became. And with her father's return, she would encounter more resistance.

That's why she decided to tell Austin the truth Saturday morning right after breakfast. Only he didn't eat breakfast. He couldn't. He was sick. Not only was his head throbbing, but his stomach was upset as well. Kacy immediately dialed her grandfather who advised her to bring him over.

On the way there Kacy wondered if this was the end of the charade. However, after spending a fair amount of time in her grandfather's examining room, Austin appeared, looking a little less green, but not angry.

"What's wrong?" she asked, jumping up.

"Looks like food poisoning to me," her grandfather answered.

"Food poisoning?"

"Austin said you ate at some little bar in the middle of nowhere last night. Had chicken sitting out on a buffet all night." He gave Kacy a look of censure.

"I didn't have the chicken."

"And you're not sick," her grandfather pointed out. He lay a gentle hand on Austin's shoulder. "He'll be all right. Just going to take a little time to get it out of his system. I gave him something for the pain."

Austin didn't say much, but allowed Kacy to help him

back to the pickup. When he did speak it was to say, "Take the bumps a little easier, will you?"

"Sure." She slipped the keys into the ignition and carefully backed the truck out of the drive.

"Take me back to the bunkhouse, would you?"

"You don't want me to take care of you?" She couldn't stop the hurt his words produced.

He reached across to squeeze her hand. "I love you, but I'm better off left alone in my condition. I'll be over as soon as I'm feeling better."

She wanted to protest, but what could she say? At least she could be grateful the headache hadn't meant his memory was returning. She still had time to tell him the truth.

At least she thought she did. As she parked her truck outside the bunkhouse she noticed a strange car outside the lodge office. She didn't think much of it until later when she went up to the kitchen to get Austin some ginger ale and soda crackers.

She walked into the lobby and came face to face with a tall, pencil-thin brunette, dressed in a silk pantsuit and wearing a wide-brimmed hat that hid most of her flawless skin. Suzy stood beside her, looking as uncomfortable as a horse surrounded by flies.

"Kacy, you're back!" There was so much relief in her sister's voice she could only assume the woman was being difficult. "We've been calling all over looking for you. Dusty finally tried Granddad's…Dad's back. He's the one who told her…" she trailed off.

Kacy could have sworn her stomach dropped to her toes. She looked at the woman who was now looking daggers at her. That this was her worst nightmare was confirmed when the woman spoke.

"I'm Daphne Delattre. I'm looking for my fiancé, Austin Bennett. I believe you know where he is."

Chapter Twelve

Kacy was certain every ounce of blood drained out of her face. "I believe I told you when you phoned I couldn't help you, Ms. Delattre."

Daphne looked down her skinny nose at Kacy. Although at five foot seven Kacy had never considered herself petite, next to this woman she felt small. It was no wonder. Daphne Delattre had to be well over six feet tall. Of course several of those inches came from the precarious high heels she wore. If she wore them around Austin she would have to look down that skinny nose at him, too.

The thought of this woman clinging to Austin's side gave Kacy a bad feeling. A really bad feeling. Daphne Delattre was cold and calculating. It was there in her eyes. True, she was beautiful, but she was the kind who would always place importance on who had worn what at which particular society event. Kacy wondered what it was about her that had attracted a man like Austin.

She thought it best if she didn't find out the answer to that question. The Austin she had fallen in love with was not the Austin this woman claimed as her personal property.

"I haven't forgotten our phone conversation," Daphne said with a haughty impatience.

"So why did you come all this way to see me?" Kacy asked calmly.

"I didn't come to see you. I came to find my fiancé."

Kacy wanted to shout at her, "He's not your fiancé. Never was, never will be," but she held her tongue. "And what makes you think you'll find him around here?"

"When Austin didn't come home and he didn't call, I did what any smart woman would have done in my position. I hired a private investigator to find him."

Kacy felt as if she were in the chute on the back of the biggest, baddest bull in the rodeo waiting for the gate to open. In a blink of an eye she could get stomped to bits, only it wouldn't be a bull doing the stomping but this glamour girl's high heels.

"And this private investigator led you to believe he's in North Dakota." She was surprised at how even she managed to keep her tone.

"At this ranch."

Kacy was about to deny the fact when the front door to the lodge opened. The chute had been opened, the bull was twisting and spinning and she was hanging on for dear life because coming right at her was Austin.

"Ohmigosh!"

Suzy's exclamation was nothing compared to the panic bubbling in Kacy's chest. She was going down and no amount of rolling would cushion her fall.

Austin gave Daphne a passing glance, dismissing her as someone whose presence needn't concern him. He walked straight over to Kacy and said, "I don't know what it was your grandfather gave me, but it worked. I came to tell you forget the soda crackers and ginger ale.

I'm hungry enough to eat real food.'' He gave her a grin that any other time would have caused her to grin right back.

However, Kacy found herself speechless. Daphne wasn't. She rushed over to give Austin a hug—not a ''I love you you're my fiancé'' kind of hug, but a ''be careful so you don't spoil my makeup and hair'' kind of hug.

''Darling, I've missed you.'' She pushed him back to arms' length and said, ''What are you doing in those clothes? You look ridiculous.''

Austin took a step backward and eyed her suspiciously. ''What's going on?''

''What's going on?'' she repeated in exaggerated disbelief. ''Is that any way to greet me after I canceled a shoot in Hawaii just to be here with you?''

He gave her the blank look Kacy had come to associate with his amnesia. ''You know me?''

''Of course I know you.'' Then she took a step back, her face losing a bit of its arrogance. ''Darling, you're frightening me. Why are you behaving like this?''

''Because he has amnesia.'' Kacy couldn't stand by and say nothing.

''Amnesia?'' Then she laughed, a brittle little laugh that sent Kacy's already frazzled nerves skittering. ''Why would you have amnesia?'' Before he could answer she said, ''I know you've been under a lot of pressure, especially where your father's concerned, but you don't need to pretend you have amnesia. I'm sure if you asked for some time off he'd give it to you.''

Austin continued to stare at her, not saying a word.

''He's not pretending,'' Kacy said quietly. ''He was hit on the head during a robbery.''

Daphne gasped, then immediately found her composure. "Oh my poor darling," she crooned, giving him another superficial hug. Then she examined the back of his head. "There's not a scar, is there?" Satisfied that he wasn't permanently disfigured she stood back and appraised him from head to toe. "A robbery! No wonder you're dressed like a cowboy. They took your clothes, too."

"He picked out those clothes himself," Suzy spoke up.

Daphne looked at Austin. "Did you?" When he nodded, she added, "Well, if you can't remember..." She let the subject drop and asked Kacy, "Has he seen a doctor?"

"Of course."

"I don't understand why you didn't call me. You had my telephone number and you knew I was anxious about him." She fixed Kacy with a glare that could have caused flowers to wilt.

"I..." Kacy began only to find nothing would come out. She turned to Austin, who just like Daphne, was staring at her with a mixture of anger and bewilderment.

"Do the Bennetts know this has happened?" Daphne continued to interrogate her, unaware of the looks being exchanged between Kacy and Austin.

"Who are the Bennetts?" Austin asked.

Daphne looked accusingly at Kacy. "Didn't you tell him his name?"

"I know my name. It's Austin Beaumont."

Daphne gasped again, covering her mouth with her perfectly manicured hand. "Oh my goodness! Poor Henry. He's probably worried sick!" Then seeing the puzzled look on Austin's face said, "You're Austin Bennett, son of Henry Bennett of Bennett Industries. Your mother died when you were quite young, but your father is alive.''

His eyes narrowed as he looked at Kacy. ''You told me my name was Beaumont.''

''She told you that?'' Daphne's face twisted in displeasure as she confronted Kacy. ''Why would you do such a thing when you knew all along who he was? The man's sick and you don't even call his family?'' She clicked her tongue in admonition.

Kacy didn't need to look at Austin to see the disappointment on his face. She could feel it, as if it were a tangible force reaching out and sticking a knife in her heart. She wanted to reach out and touch him, to wipe away the confusion and the disillusionment that had changed his handsome features into a mask she didn't recognize. But she couldn't because the look in his eye warned her not to get near.

''Is she right? Did you know how to contact my family before she arrived?'' he asked.

''Yes, I did know but it's not what you think. It's a long, complicated story and...''

He turned his back on her, not waiting to hear her explanation. Instead he asked Daphne, ''Where do I live?''

''Chicago. On the gold coast of Lake Michigan.''

''I have a boat?''

''Yes.'' Her eyes sparkled with hope. ''Are you starting to remember?''

''No.'' The answer was curt.

She put her arm through his. ''It's all right, darling. We'll take you to a doctor. A *good* doctor. All that matters is that I've found you.''

The way she was fussing over him made Kacy want to gag.

Austin didn't look very comfortable with the attention, either. "And you are?"

"Oh my. You really do have amnesia." Her features softened—at least as much as it was possible for them to move beneath layers of makeup. "Darling, I'm Daphne. Your fiancée."

Austin looked stunned. "We're engaged to be married?"

"Of course." She laughed nervously. "It's a good thing you have amnesia or I might be offended by that question."

He looked totally confused to Kacy. "I don't remember."

"Of course you don't, but you will in time. What you need is to come home. To familiar surroundings."

Kacy wanted him to tell Daphne he wasn't going anywhere, but he didn't. What he did do was gently remove her arm from his. "I need to get my things."

"You're leaving?" Kacy knew the bull had kicked her but good. She was flying through the air with nothing to cling to for help. "Austin, you're not leaving, are you?" she called out to him.

He paid no attention to her. Without a word he turned and marched out of the lodge. She ran after him, pleading for him to listen. "Austin, wait. Please listen to me. I had my reasons for not saying anything."

"I don't want to hear your reasons." He walked so fast she was forced to run to keep up with him. "You lied to me, made me think I was someone else. I don't know how you could do that when you knew what it meant to me to unravel the mystery of my past."

"I'm sorry, Austin. I was wrong and now what seemed like a good idea at the time sounds like the most stupid thing in the whole world, but what happened between us was good. And that never would have happened if..."

He had reached the bunkhouse and went inside, slamming the door on her explanation. She swallowed her pride, fought back the tears and went in after him. He took the few items of clothing he owned from the foot locker and threw them on the bed in a pile.

"Austin, can't you at least look at me?" she begged as he worked without so much as a glance in her direction.

He acted as if she wasn't even in the room with him. He disappeared into the bathroom only to come out carrying an armload of personal care items. When a can of shaving cream fell to the floor, Kacy automatically stooped to pick it up.

"Please don't leave like this, Austin," she begged as she handed it to him.

He grabbed it from her, his eyes flashing with anger, then tossed it on the bed with the rest of his things. When everything he owned lay in the center of the bunk, he stopped and faced Kacy.

"Look." He pointed to the pile. "There it is. The entire net worth of Austin Beaumont. Pretty pitiful, isn't it? But what's even more pitiful is that I was stupid enough to believe it."

"Austin, will you please listen to me? I can explain," she began only to have him cut her off.

"There are no explanations for this."

The clicking of heels announced Daphne's arrival in the bunkhouse. "Oh my! Don't tell me this is where they made you sleep?" Her eyes made a survey of the room, grimacing at its starkness. Seeing the stuff on the bed she asked, "Do you have a suitcase?"

"Don't need one." He started toward the door. "I'm ready when you are."

"Then we should be on our way." Daphne didn't waste any time getting out of the bunkhouse.

As Austin headed for the door, Kacy called out to him, "Aren't you going to take your things?"

"They don't belong to me. You're the one who created Austin Beaumont. You keep them," he said, then tossed his hat on the pile before pushing the screen door open.

Kacy watched him leave. She hadn't fallen to the ground and been stomped on by the bull. She managed to drag her dejected body over to the door in time to see Austin climb into the front seat of Daphne's rental car.

In a matter of minutes the car was gone and all that was left was a cloud of dust. "I was going to tell you," Kacy muttered with a hopelessness to the departing vehicle.

She turned and saw Austin's belongings piled on the bed. A tear rolled down her cheek. Then another. And another. Among the articles of clothing was the fancy white dancing shirt. She snatched it from the pile and brought it close to her chest. It still smelled of his aftershave and sent a wave of longing through her.

"Kace, are you okay?" The screen door creaked as Suzy stepped inside.

Kacy stuffed the white shirt in the bottom of the pile and brushed her palms across her cheeks to erase the tears. "I'm fine," she lied, refusing to let her sister know just how badly she hurt inside.

"You're not crying, are you?" the younger woman asked, walking cautiously toward her sister.

"If I am it's because I'm mad. Did you see the way that Delattre woman looked down her nose at us? No wonder the Austin Bennett who tried to cheat us out of the money was such a cold, arrogant man."

"But this Austin seemed different," Suzy noted.

"He was different," Kacy said quietly, fighting back the urge to cry.

"Now what?"

"Now we go back to life as it was before Austin Bennett ever stepped foot on the ranch." She got up to get a box from the storage area of the bunkhouse. She set it on the floor and transferred Austin's belongings from the bed to the box.

"What are you going to do with that stuff?"

Kacy shrugged. "Maybe burn it."

Suzy's eyebrows raised. "No! You should at least donate it to the church clothing drive."

"I suppose you're right." When everything was in the box, Kacy hefted it to her hip and carried it out to the pickup. She didn't take it to the incinerator, nor did she drive into town and drop it off at the church. She drove home, carried it up the stairs and put it in her studio loft.

AUSTIN STARED OUT the window at the Chicago city streets. He had been back for almost two weeks and still nothing looked familiar. Not his brownstone on Astor Avenue, not his office at Bennett Industries, not even the man who called himself his father.

He was like a tourist in a city he was supposed to know well, having to ask directions everywhere he went. Despite being examined by several top neurologists in the field of memory loss, he was still without his memory. Every doctor said the same thing. "Give it some time, Austin."

Time, Austin had discovered, was a strange force. Why was it that two weeks at the Triple J could make him feel as if he had found a sense of identity yet he had been in Chicago two weeks and he still couldn't find anything to make him feel as if he belonged?

He went over to the tower of CDs next to the stereo system and searched through the titles. Up one row. Down another. Nothing interested him. The one he wanted wasn't there. k.d. lang. He closed his eyes and memories of the first night he spent with Kacy played in his mind. The sheer fabric of her blouse, the long broomstick skirt, the satin bra he had found on the ground, the satin bikini briefs he had tossed to the floor.

A rush of blood made him ache for her. He opened his eyes hoping to erase those vivid memories, but it didn't help. How ironic it was that the parts of his life he wanted to remember remain locked away in his brain, yet the stuff he wanted to forget haunted him.

He poured himself a drink and sat down in his entertainment room. With a push of a button his projection screen TV was on. With the rhythm of a machine gun he used the remote control to change channels, surfing for what, he wasn't sure. Sitcoms, dramas, talk shows…he went through them all, stopping only when he saw a cowboy riding a bull. It was the movie *8 Seconds*. It was filled with cowboys and cowgirls, which only made him think about a particular cowgirl who had been brave enough to ride a bull but hadn't been able to tell him the truth.

Why had she lied to him? Why had she pretended he was just another cowboy when she knew all along that he was Austin Bennett of Bennett Industries? These were questions that continued to torment him no matter how hard he tried to put them out of his mind.

When the phone rang, he didn't answer it. A female voice activated the answering machine. He heard

Daphne leave her usual message, "Darling, I hope you're not just sitting there refusing to answer the phone. I want you to come to dinner with me this evening at the Brentwoods. Please say yes. It will be so good for you. You need to be with your friends. That's the only way you'll recover your memory."

Austin heaved a sigh of relief when she finally ended her message. He wished she would just leave him alone. As hard as she tried to put things back the way they were in his life, it wasn't working. The harder she tried, the more irritated he became. He wondered what kind of man he had been to get involved with such a woman.

Actually, everything would have been much easier if he only had feelings for Daphne. His father would be happy. Daphne would be happy. The problem was, he wouldn't be happy. Because as hard as he tried to feel something for the beautiful model, he couldn't.

Life just wasn't fair. He looked around him and saw everything that should make a man happy. A successful career, a prestigious home, a beautiful woman. Austin Bennett didn't lack for money, friends or social position. He had it all. Only the *all* he had didn't interest him.

Again he sighed. It was because of Kacy Judd. How could he love someone who was dishonest? And why didn't he care whether or not he had any of the fancy trimmings that came with being Austin Bennett of Bennett Industries?

Maybe because he couldn't remember Austin Bennett. But he knew Austin Beaumont quite well. And it was Austin Beaumont who would gladly settle for a steady job on a ranch if it meant having Kacy at his side.

Austin groaned. Was he pathetic or what? All he could hope for was that when his memory returned he would forget all about his sojourn in North Dakota.

"WHAT BRINGS YOU HERE? You're not sick, are you?" Kacy's grandfather asked when she hopped out of her pickup.

"I brought you some baked carrot crispies for Lulubelle," she answered, handing him a bag filled with the muffin treats.

He opened the sack and peered inside. "Smell almost good enough to eat myself. Shame to waste them on an old nag like Lulubelle."

"That's why you need to feed them to her. She's old and she needs a little TLC."

"Don't we all," he said, shoving his arm through hers and steering her toward the house. "Come on inside and you can tell me why you're really here."

Kacy gave her grandfather's arm a playful punch. "I'm here because I want to see you."

"Uh-huh." He opened the back door and motioned for her to step into the kitchen. "You can fool some of the people some of the time..." he trailed off. Once inside, he set the muffins on the counter, then reached into the refrigerator and pulled out a pitcher of lemonade.

As soon as he had poured them each a glass, he sat down across from Kacy at the table and asked, "So are you going to tell me what's putting those dark circles under your eyes?"

Kacy sighed. It was true. She hadn't come to see her granddad just because of the muffins. She needed to talk to someone about Austin and he was the only one she knew would understand.

"I made a big mistake," she confessed.

"I guess you're talking about Austin, aren't you?"

She nodded miserably. "You heard what happened."

He neither confirmed or denied hearing anything. "You're in love with him, aren't you?"

"Granddad! I've only known him a few weeks," she protested.

"That doesn't mean anything. I knew the moment I laid eyes on your grandma that she would be the only woman for me."

"That was different. You didn't have amnesia."

"Is Austin still without his memory?"

She shrugged. "That's what I don't know. I was hoping that maybe you could find out for me." When she could see he was going to protest she quickly added, "You were his doctor of record here. You could call the clinic in New York and get a medical report."

"Which I couldn't share with you because that's privileged information," he reminded her sternly.

"But..." she trailed off, losing any hope that she'd ever hear anything at all ever again about Austin Bennett. At the possibility, a tear trickled down her cheek. She swiped at it with the back of her hand, but not before her grandfather saw.

He reached for her hands and covered them with his large, gnarly ones. "Listen to me, Granddaughter. Only you can resolve this."

"Me? How can I when he won't talk to me?"

"Sure he will."

She sniffled. "Uh-uh. I've tried calling dozens of times and all I get is an answering machine. I leave messages but he never returns them."

"So you've given up?"

"He hates me," she said in a near whisper.

"That wasn't hate I saw in his eyes when the two of you were here," her grandfather said consolingly.

"That was before he found out..." she trailed off. She

reached into her pocket for a tissue and blew her nose. "The worst part is he wouldn't even listen to my explanation."

"Then it's about time he does. My advice to you is this. Go see him." He emphasized each word with a jab of his finger on the tabletop.

"I can't," she said quietly.

"Can't?" Her grandfather practically bellowed the word. "Are you telling me that you've got the guts to ride a bull, you've got the guts to break a horse, yet you're afraid to face one man you love?"

When she didn't answer right away he said, "Well? Are those Judd genes inside that skinny little body or not? Because you ought to know that Judds go after what they want in life."

"You're right," she answered, lifting her chin. "They do. And they usually get it, don't they?"

"You're darn tootin' they do."

She downed the remainder of her lemonade, thumping her glass on the table when it was gone. "Good. Cuz I'm going to Chicago. Today."

AUSTIN DIDN'T SEE much point in going back to work, but his father seemed to think it would be some sort of therapy. So he went in to the office each morning and did a pile of paperwork which he had a feeling was normally done by his secretary but now was being delegated to him in hopes of stirring some activity in his memory.

Of all the people he had met since his return to Chicago, his secretary Jean was the one who was the most understanding. With her gentle touch and her unlimited patience, she made each day at Bennett Industries tolerable. She filled him in on as much of his background as was possible. It didn't take Austin long to recognize that Jean had been more than a secretary to him. She had been a friend.

She was also a great sentry, protecting his inner sanctum from unwanted visitors. Such as Daphne. It was because of Jean that Austin had learned that Daphne was not his fiancée. Unfortunately, his secretary couldn't say just how important the model was in his life, but she was certain no marriage proposal had been issued.

During the short time Austin had been back in Chicago, he had come to trust and value Jean's opinion. He turned to her often for help with his work and whenever she announced that he had a visitor, he always asked her whether or not it was someone he needed to see.

That was why when she marched into his office and announced that there was a Kacy Judd waiting to see him, he automatically asked, "What for?"

"She says she owes you some money."

"Tell her she owes me nothing," he said uneasily.

"I don't know this woman, Austin. I'm really not comfortable passing along that message," Jean told him. "Shall I bring her in?"

"No. Yes."

"Which is it, Austin?" she asked gently.

"You know that woman I told you about in North Dakota? The one who had ridden a bull?" Jean nodded. "Well, that's her."

A smile spread across his secretary's face. "Well, then that does it. Of course you're going to see her," she said, then gave his shoulder a gentle squeeze. "She came a long way to see you."

Austin wanted to tell Jean that she was a hopeless romantic if she thought anything could come of his relationship with Kacy Judd. He was convinced that he was right about that when Kacy entered the room.

Instead of western wear she wore a long skirt and a flimsy blouse—one very similar to what she'd had on that night they swam naked in the river. At the memory, his hormones started to stir. On her feet were a pair of sandals and her hair hung in curls around her face. To Austin she had never looked more beautiful.

She didn't smile when she saw him, but eyed him cautiously. "Hello, Austin."

"Kacy."

She pulled an envelope from her straw purse and offered it to him. "I brought you the money you earned as an employee of the ranch."

He held up his hands, palms outward. "Keep it. I don't want it and I don't need it."

"That doesn't matter. The Judds aren't like the Bennetts. They pay their debts." She tried to stuff the envelope in his pocket, but he grabbed her by the wrist and held her firmly in his grasp.

"What kind of a statement is that?"

"Just what I said. We pay money we owe, unlike Bennett Industries." She continued to struggle until he released her wrist. Then she tossed the brown envelope onto his desk. "There. Consider our debt paid."

She started to walk away, but he stopped her. "Wait. I want you to explain what you meant by that remark about Bennetts not paying their debts."

"Are you sure you want to know the truth? You didn't want to give me a chance to explain the last time we were together," she reminded him.

The memory of their last meeting sent an ache through him. "Are you going to tell me what you mean or not?" he asked impatiently.

"You brought fourteen employees to the Triple J for a week-long seminar on team building. At the end of the week, you left. Despite a consensus by your employees that the seminar was indeed a success, you determined it wasn't and refused to pay my family one half of the money you owed us."

Austin took a moment to absorb what she said. "Are you saying you allowed me to believe I was a ranch hand in order to collect on a debt my family owed your ranch?"

She nodded solemnly. "It seemed like a good idea at the time. You owed us a lot of money."

He slumped back against the desk, trying to comprehend the chain of events that had led him to this point in his life. "So you didn't tell anyone I was there because you wanted to get revenge."

"It wasn't revenge. It was what we were due. You've seen our ranch, you've seen how we live. We can't afford people not to pay for services they've already received."

"What did you think would happen when my memory returned?"

"You'd leave. What I didn't expect was that I'd fall in love with you."

He chuckled without humor. "Some love," he said sarcastically.

"Look. You can tell me I made a big mistake. You can tell me it was stupid to try to recoup the money in such a way. But you're not going to tell me I didn't fall in love with you."

Her eyes were flashing now, darkening to an emerald green and reminding Austin of how they looked when her passion was aroused. He wanted to take her in his arms and tell her he didn't care that she had lied to him.

He wanted to kiss her until she promised never to ever lie to him again.

But he couldn't. Something stopped him. He raked a hand through his hair. "All right. You've said what you've come to say. You've given me the money. You can go."

She stared at him, her face a picture of hurt and disappointment. "Is that all you have to say to me? Doesn't what happened between us mean anything to you?"

His chest felt so heavy he was having difficulty breathing. "It does mean something to me. But I'm a man without a memory, Kacy. I can't make promises to you or any other woman as long as my entire life history is four weeks old."

She came closer to him. "I told you, Austin, that I don't care about your past. I'm in love with the man you are today. I don't think that man is going to change even if your memory *does* come back."

The temptation to take her into his arms and kiss was almost overwhelming. As he stared at her pretty little face, he knew that she was right. That no matter what her reasons were for keeping his identity from him, they didn't change the fact that they had found something truly special. Before he could tell her, however, the door flew open and in came Daphne.

"Darling! Have you forgotten our lunch date?" She took one look at Kacy and said, "You'll have to excuse us. We're supposed to be meeting his father to discuss wedding plans."

Kacy was out of his office faster than a speeding bullet. "Damn you, Daphne!" Austin shouted at her, then ran after Kacy.

But he was too late. She stepped into the elevator seconds before the door slid shut. Trying to catch her,

Austin took the stairs, running down ten flights as if he were an athlete racing for a gold medal. As he reached the ground level, he saw the back of Kacy slipping through the mass of people going in and out of the busy office building.

Austin went after her, through the revolving door and down the crowded sidewalk. She ran across the street on a "Don't Walk" light. Dodging traffic he tried to catch up to her but he met with an immovable force. A car. He fell to the ground and into darkness.

Chapter Thirteen

Austin awoke in a hospital. His father was at his side. Daphne hovered in the background.

"He's awake!" he heard his father declare jubilantly.

Within seconds a nurse entered the room, fussing over him, asking him all sorts of questions, shooing his guests out into the hallway so that she could check his vital signs.

"Can you hear me, Mr. Bennett?" she asked when they were alone.

"Loud and clear," he answered the woman in white.

"Do you remember what happened to you?"

"I was hit by a car trying to catch my girlfriend. Is she here?"

"You must mean Daphne Delattre, the model. Oh yes, she's here," the nurse answered cheerfully. "I understand she's your fiancée. You're a lucky man. She's quite lovely."

"No. I'm looking for a cowgirl." He blinked, as the room spun slightly. "A redheaded cowgirl." At the thought that Kacy might still be out there on the streets of Chicago needing his protection, he tried to rise.

The nurse gently pushed him back down. "You just stay put, Mr. Bennett. You've had a nasty blow to the head and you're not thinking clearly. Why don't I send your fiancée in to cheer you up?''

He wanted to repeat that Daphne was not his fiancée, but everything was so fuzzy. He was drowsy...so drowsy. Again he opened his eyes, but his lids were too heavy to keep them open.

When he heard his father's voice he said, "Dad. Everything's going to be okay. I know who I am.''

Then he fell back to sleep.

KACY STOPPED EATING at the lodge. Unless it was a required session where her attendance was mandatory, she preferred to spend her free time alone. After everything that had happened this summer, she found it difficult to be around her family. She had made a fool of herself over Austin and needed some time away from the others to collect her thoughts.

Ever since she had been back from Chicago she had told herself that she was over Austin. He was just another man. Men came and went in her life. So what else was new? This one had had a strike against him to start. It shouldn't have surprised her that the relationship had come to a dead end with a bang.

One good thing had come out of her trip to Chicago. A check for the balance of the money owed by Bennett Industries arrived in the mail the following week. That had pleased her family. But though Kacy would never have admitted it, she would gladly have traded the money for Austin Beaumont.

Only she needed to keep reminding herself that Austin Beaumont didn't exist. Just Austin Bennett. And it was obvious that Daphne Delattre had her hooks into him. Whenever Kacy got a little weepy over losing Austin, she thought about that week he had spent at the lodge.

CEO Austin had been arrogant, demanding and downright difficult. Not at all the kind of man she needed in her life.

After weeks of mooning around her cottage, she decided the time had come to get over the man. She called up her sister and asked if she wanted to go to the Buckle Bar for a few beers. They went, had a good time, danced a few dances. But the whole time Kacy couldn't stop thinking about what it had been like when she and Austin had visited the bar.

After dropping Suzy at home, Kacy headed back to her cottage. Even from a distance she could see that the light was on. She figured one of her brothers must have been waiting up for her. As she pulled into the drive, she saw a shiny red pickup out front.

Carefully, she climbed out of the truck. As she neared the porch she heard a voice say, ''I see you still like to live dangerously. Your doors are unlocked.''

It was Austin. He sat on the porch swing, wearing jeans, a western shirt and a cowboy hat.

''What are you doing here?'' Kacy asked from a distance.

''I brought you a present.'' He gestured toward the drive.

''The truck?''

''Yup. I figured it's about time you put old Bertha to rest.''

Kacy was speechless. She examined the shiny new pickup, inside and out, at least as best she could in the dark. Finally, she asked, ''Why would you buy me a truck?''

''Because I love you.''

Kacy wasted no time running up onto the porch. He

waited with open arms, kissing her until they were both breathless.

"What about Daphne?" she asked, tracing his mouth with her fingertips.

"I never was going to marry Daphne. And I do mean *never.*"

"You can remember?"

"Everything. Riding Old Yellow, camping at the river, kissing you..." He grinned, a sly sexy grin that held a promise of passion.

"It was a crazy five days, wasn't it?" she reflected wistfully.

"I didn't behave very well, but I want you to know I never intended not to pay the money Bennett Industries owed you. I was just going to make you sweat about it a couple of days, then mail you the check."

"But you got off the airplane. You weren't going back to Chicago."

"Because I realized how petty it was for me to with- hold the money. I did a lot of thinking that morning I left here. I realize that I didn't have what I wanted in life. I wasn't sure even what it was that I wanted, but I just knew I needed to look for it."

"Your secretary said you were taking a vacation."

"I hadn't really thought that far ahead. All I knew was that I didn't want to go back to Chicago and I had to pay the money I owed your family," he explained. "Only I was robbed on my way back to the ranch with the check."

"Is it true they caught the guys?"

Austin nodded. "Bill Cox told me they tried to cash that check made out to the Triple J somewhere in Wy- oming."

She sighed. "If it weren't for them, we wouldn't be together."

He shrugged. "Who knows? I was on my way back to the ranch, don't forget."

She studied his face. "We fought a lot those first five days," she reminded him.

"But we got along beautifully those next two weeks." He tipped her chin up and held her eyes. "Kacy, I believe Austin Beaumont and Austin Bennett are the same person. A bump on the head doesn't change a person, it just makes him look at life a little differently."

"Why did Daphne say you were discussing wedding plans that day I came to your office?"

"She knew I was in love with you. While I was a guest here at the lodge, she had phoned. Well, during our conversation I called her by your name. You see, even though I didn't want to admit it, I was falling in love with you back then."

"I felt the same way. I was attracted to you, yet I didn't know why." She kissed him lightly, then leaned her head on his shoulder.

"That day Daphne walked in on us I was about to tell you that it didn't matter whether my memory ever came back because I loved you, too. Only she walked in, you raced out, and I got hit by a car."

"What?" she exclaimed in alarm, sitting up straight.

He explained about the accident and his stay in the hospital. When he was done she examined every inch of his face asking, "Are you sure you're okay?"

"I will be if you say I can stay."

"For how long?"

"I don't know…how long do you think you can stand having a city slicker like me hanging around the place?"

"Since I like to live dangerously…hmm let me see."

"How about a lifetime?"

"Are you serious?"

He pulled a velvet box from his pocket. Inside was a diamond solitaire.

One look into his eyes and Kacy knew the answer to her question.

If you enjoyed what you just read,
then we've got an offer you can't resist!

Take 2 bestselling love stories FREE!

Plus get a FREE surprise gift!

HEART OF THE WEST

Every Man Has His Price!

Lost Springs Ranch was
famous for turning young
mavericks into good men.
So word that the ranch was
in financial trouble sent
a herd of loyal bachelors
stampeding back to
Wyoming to put themselves
on the auction block!